MY BEAUTIFUL LAUNDRETTE
and other writings

HANIF KUREISHI

My Beautiful Laundrette
and other writings

faber and faber

This volume first published in Great Britain in 1996
by Faber and Faber Limited
3 Queen Square London WC1N 3AU

My Beautiful Laundrette and *The Rainbow Sign* first published in 1986
by Faber and Faber Limited
Eight Arms to Hold You first published in *London Kills Me* in 1991
by Faber and Faber Limited
Bradford first published in *Granta 20* in winter 1986
Wild Women, Wild Men first published in *Granta 39* in spring 1992
Finishing the Job first published in *New Statesman & Society* in October 1988

Photoset by Parker Typesetting Service, Leicester
Printed in England by Clays Ltd, St Ives plc

Hanif Kureishi is hereby identified as author of this work
in accordance with Section 77 of the Copyright,
Designs and Patents Act 1988

A CIP record for this book
is available from the British Library
ISBN 0–571–17738–7

2 4 6 8 10 9 7 5 3 1

CONTENTS

My Beautiful Laundrette

INTRODUCTION

I wrote the script of *My Beautiful Laundrette* in my uncle's house in Karachi, Pakistan, in February 1985, during the night. As I wrote, cocks crowed and the call to prayer reverberated through crackly speakers from a nearby mosque. It was impossible to sleep. One morning as I sat on the verandah having breakfast, I had a phone call from Howard Davies, a director with the Royal Shakespeare Company, with whom I'd worked twice before. He wanted to direct Brecht's *Mother Courage*, with Judi Dench in the lead role. He wanted me to adapt it.

That summer, back in England and at Howard's place in Stratford-upon-Avon, I sat in the orchard with two pads of paper in front of me: on one I rewrote *My Beautiful Laundrette* and on the other I adapted Brecht from a literal translation into language that could be spoken by the RSC actors.

As *Laundrette* was the first film I'd written, and I was primarily a playwright, I wrote each scene of the film like a little scene for a play, with the action written like stage directions and with lots of dialogue. Then I'd cut most of the dialogue and add more stage directions, often set in cars, or with people running about, to keep the thing moving, since films required action.

I'd had a couple of lunches with Karin Banborough of Channel Four. She wanted me to write something for *Film on Four*. I was extremely keen. For me *Film on Four* had taken over from the BBC's *Play For Today* in presenting serious contemporary drama on TV to a wide audience. The work of TV writers like Alan Bennett (much of it directed by Stephen Frears), Dennis Potter, Harold Pinter, Alan Plater and David Mercer, influenced me greatly when I was young and living at home in the suburbs. On my way up to London the morning after a *Play For Today* I'd sit in the train listening to people discussing the previous night's drama and interrupt them with my own opinions.

The great advantage of TV drama was the people watched it; difficult, challenging things could be said about contemporary life. The theatre, despite the efforts of touring companies and so

3

on, has failed to get its ideas beyond a small enthusiastic audience.

When I finished a draft of *My Beautiful Laundrette*, and *Mother Courage* had gone into rehearsal, Karin Banborough, David Rose and I discussed directors for the film.

A couple of days later I went to see a friend, David Gothard, who was then running Riverside Studios. I often went for a walk by the river in the early evening, and then I'd sit in David's office. He always had the new books and the latest magazines; and whoever was appearing at Riverside would be around. Riverside stood for tolerance, scepticism and intelligence. The feeling there was that works of art, plays, books and so on, were important. This is a rare thing in England. For many writers, actors, dancers and artists, Riverside was what a university should be: a place to learn and talk and work and meet your contemporaries. There was no other place like it in London and David Gothard was the great encourager, getting work on and introducing people to one another.

He suggested I ask Stephen Frears to direct the film. I thought this an excellent idea, except that I admired Frears too much to have the nerve to ring him. David Gothard did this and I cycled to Stephen's house in Notting Hill, where he lived in a street known as 'director's row' because of the number of film directors living there.

He said he wanted to shoot my film in February. As it was November already I pointed out that February might be a little soon. Would there be time to prepare, to rewrite? But he had a theory: when you have a problem, he said, bring things forward; do them sooner rather than later. And anyway, February was a good month for him; he made his best films then; England looked especially unpleasant; and people worked faster in the cold.

The producers, Tim Bevan and Sarah Radclyffe, Stephen had worked with before, on promos for rock bands. So the film was set up and I started to rewrite. Stephen and I had long talks, each of us pacing up and down the same piece of carpet, in different directions.

The film started off as an epic. It was to be like *The Godfather*, opening in the past with the arrival of an immigrant family in

4

England and showing their progress to the present. There were to be many scenes set in the 1950s; people would eat bread and dripping and get off boats a lot; there would be scenes of Johnny and Omar as children and large-scale set pieces of racist marches with scenes of mass violence.

We soon decided it was impossible to make a film of such scale. That film is still to be made. Instead I set the film in the present, though references to the past remain.

It was shot in six weeks in February and March in 1985 on a low budget and 16mm film. For this I was glad. There were no commercial pressures on us, no one had a lot of money invested in the film who would tell us what to do. And I was tired of seeing lavish films set in exotic locations; it seemed to me that anyone could make such films, providing they had an old book, a hot country, new technology and were capable of aiming the camera at an attractive landscape in the hot country in front of which stood a star in a perfectly clean costume delivering lines from the old book.

We decided the film was to have gangster and thriller elements, since the gangster film is the form that corresponds most closely to the city, with its gangs and violence. And the film was to be an amusement, despite its references to racism, unemployment and Thatcherism. Irony is the modern mode, a way of commenting on bleakness and cruelty without falling into dourness and didacticism. And ever since the first time I heard people in a theatre laugh during a play of mine, I've wanted it to happen again and again.

We found actors – Saeed Jaffrey, for whom I'd written the part; and Roshan Seth I'd seen in David Hare's play *Map Of The World*, commanding that huge stage at the National with complete authority. I skidded through the snow to see Shirley Ann Field and on arriving at her flat was so delighted by her charm and enthusiasm, and so ashamed of the smallness of her part, that there and then I added the material about the magic potions, the moving furniture and the walking trousers. It must have seemed that the rest of the film was quite peripheral and she would be playing the lead in a kind of 'Exorcist' movie with a gay Pakistani, a drug-dealer and a fluff-drying spin-drier in the background.

Soon we stood under railway bridges in Vauxhall at two in the morning in March; we knocked the back wall out of someone's flat and erected a platform outside to serve as the balcony of Papa's flat, which had so many railway lines dipping and criss-crossing beside and above it that inside it you shook like peas in maracas; in an old shop we built a laundrette of such authenticity that people came in off the street with their washing; and I stood on the set making up dialogue before the actors did it themselves, and added one or two new scenes.

When shooting was finished and we had about two-and-a-quarter hours of material strung together, we decided to have a showing for a group of 'wise ones'. They would be film directors, novelists and film writers who'd give us their opinions and thereby aid in editing the film. So I sat at the back of the small viewing cinema as they watched the film. We then cut forty-five minutes out.

The film played at the Edinburgh Film Festival and then went into the cinema.

The script printed here is the last draft before shooting. I haven't attempted to update it or cut out the scenes which were not used in the final version, since it may be of interest to people to compare script with film.

I must thank my friends Walter Donohue, David Gothard, Salman Rushdie, David Nokes and, of course, Sally Whitman, without whom.

My Beautiful Laundrette was first shown at the Edinburgh Film Festival in autumn 1985. The film opened at the London Film Festival on 15 November and was subsequently released at London cinemas on 16 November 1985.

The cast included:

JOHNNY	Daniel Day Lewis
GENGHIS	Richard Graham
SALIM	Derrick Branche
OMAR	Gordon Warnecke
PAPA	Roshan Seth
NASSER	Saeed Jaffrey
RACHEL	Shirley Anne Field
BILQUIS	Charu Bala Choksi
CHERRY	Souad Faress
TANIA	Rita Wolf
ZAKI	Gurdial Sira
MOOSE	Stephen Marcus
GANG MEMBER ONE	Dawn Archibald
GANG MEMBER TWO	Jonathan Moore

Photography	Oliver Stapleton
Film Editor	Mick Audsley
Designer	Hugo Luczyc Wyhowski
Sound Recordist	Albert Bailey
Music	Ludus Tonalis
Casting	Debbie McWilliams
Costume Design	Lindy Hemming
Make-up	Elaine Carew

Screenplay	Hanif Kureishi
Producers	Sarah Radclyffe and Tim Bevan
Director	Stephen Frears

EXT. OUTSIDE A LARGE DETACHED HOUSE. DAY
CHERRY *and* SALIM *get out of their car. Behind them, the* FOUR
JAMAICANS *get out of their car.*

CHERRY *and* SALIM *walk towards the house. It is a large falling-down place, in South London. It's quiet at the moment – early morning – but the ground floor windows are boarded up.*

On the boarded-up windows is painted: 'Your greed will be the death of us all' and 'We will defeat the running wogs of capitalism' and 'Opium is the opium of the unemployed'.

CHERRY *and* SALIM *look up at the house. The* FOUR JAMAICANS *stand behind them, at a respectful distance.*

CHERRY: I don't even remember buying this house at the auction. What are we going to do with it?

SALIM: Tomorrow we start to renovate it.

CHERRY: How many people are living here?

SALIM: There are no people living here. There are only squatters. And they're going to be renovated – right now.
(*And* SALIM *pushes* CHERRY *forward, giving her the key.* CHERRY *goes to the front door of the house.* SALIM, *with* TWO JAMAICANS *goes round the side of the house.* TWO JAMAICANS *go round the other side.*)

INT. A ROOM IN THE SQUAT. DAY
GENGHIS *and* JOHNNY *are living in a room in the squat. It is freezing cold, with broken windows.* GENGHIS *is asleep on a mattress, wrapped up. He has the flu.* JOHNNY *is lying frozen in a deck chair, with blankets over him. He has just woken up.*

EXT. OUTSIDE THE HOUSE. DAY
CHERRY *tries to unlock the front door of the place. But the door has been barred. She looks in through the letter box. A barricade has been erected in the hall.*

EXT. THE SIDE OF THE HOUSE. DAY
The JAMAICANS *break into the house through side windows. They*

climb in. SALIM *also climbs into the house.*

INT. INSIDE THE HOUSE. DAY
The JAMAICANS *and* SALIM *are in the house now.*
   The JAMAICANS *are kicking open the doors of the squatted rooms. The* SQUATTERS *are unprepared, asleep or half-awake, in disarray.*
   The JAMAICANS *are going from room to room, yelling for everyone to leave now or get thrown out of the windows with their belongings.*
   Some SQUATTERS *complain but they are shoved out of their rooms into the hall; or down the stairs.* SALIM *is eager about all of this.*

INT. GENGHIS AND JOHNNY'S ROOM. DAY
JOHNNY *looks up the corridor to see what's happening. He goes back into the room quickly and starts stuffing his things into a black plastic bag. He is shaking* GENGHIS *at the same time.*
GENGHIS: I'm ill.
JOHNNY: We're moving house.
GENGHIS: No, we've got to fight.
JOHNNY: Too early in the morning.
   (*He rips the blankets off* GENGHIS, *who lies there fully dressed, coughing and shivering. A* JAMAICAN *bursts into the room.*)
   All right, all right.
   (*The* JAMAICAN *watches a moment as* GENGHIS, *too weak to resist, but cursing violently, takes the clothes* JOHNNY *shoves at him and follows* JOHNNY *to the window.* JOHNNY *opens the broken window.*)

EXT. OUTSIDE THE HOUSE. DAY
A wide shot of the house.
   The SQUATTERS *are leaving through windows and the re-opened front door and gathering in the front garden, arranging their wretched belongings. Some of them are junkies. They look dishevelled and disheartened.*
   From an upper room in the house come crashing a guitar, a TV and some records. This is followed by the enquiring head of a JAMAICAN, *looking to see these have hit no one.*
   One SQUATTER, *in the front garden, is resisting and a* JAMAICAN *is holding him. The* SQUATTER *screams at* CHERRY: *you pig, you scum, you filthy rich shit, etc.*

As SALIM *goes to join* CHERRY, *she goes to the screaming* SQUATTER *and gives him a hard backhander across the face.*

EXT. THE BACK OF THE HOUSE. DAY
JOHNNY *and* GENGHIS *stumble down through the back garden of the house and over the wall at the end,* JOHNNY *pulling and helping the exhausted* GENGHIS.

At no time do they see CHERRY *or* SALIM.

INT. BATHROOM. DAY
OMAR *has been soaking Papa's clothes in the bath. He pulls them dripping from the bath and puts them in an old steel bucket, wringing them out. He picks up the bucket.*

EXT. BALCONY. DAY
OMAR *is hanging out Papa's dripping pjyamas on the washing line on the balcony, pulling them out of the bucket.*

The balcony overlooks several busy railway lines, commuter routes into Charing Cross and London Bridge, from the suburbs.

OMAR *turns and looks through the glass of the balcony door into the main room of the flat.* PAPA *is lying in bed. He pours himself some vodka. Water from the pyjamas drips down Omar's trousers and into his shoes.*

When he turns away, a train, huge, close, fast, crashes towards the camera and bangs and rattles its way past, a few feet from the exposed overhanging balcony. OMAR *is unperturbed.*

INT. PAPA'S ROOM. DAY
The flat OMAR *and his father,* PAPA, *share in South London. It's a small, damp and dirty place which hasn't been decorated for years.*

PAPA *is as thin as a medieval Christ: an unkempt alcoholic. His hair is long; his toenails uncut; he is unshaven and scratches his arse shamelessly. Yet he is not without dignity.*

His bed is in the living room. PAPA *never leaves the bed and watches TV most of the time.*

By the bed is a photograph of Papa's dead wife, Mary. And on the bed is an address book and the telephone.

PAPA *empties the last of a bottle of vodka into a filthy glass. He rolls the empty bottle under the bed.*

OMAR *is now pushing an old-fashioned and ineffective carpet sweeper across the floor.* PAPA *looks at* OMAR*'s face. He indicates that* OMAR *should move his face closer, which* OMAR *reluctantly does. To amuse himself,* PAPA *squashes* OMAR*'s nose and pulls his cheeks, shaking the boy's unamused face from side to side.*

PAPA: I'm fixing you with a job. With your uncle. Work now, till you go back to college. If your face gets any longer here you'll overbalance. Or I'll commit suicide.

INT. KITCHEN. DAY

OMAR *is in the kitchen of the flat, stirring a big saucepan of dall. He can see through the open door his* FATHER *speaking on the phone to* NASSER. PAPA *speaks in Urdu. 'How are you?' he says. 'And Bilquis? And Tania and the other girls?'*

PAPA: (*Into phone*) Can't you give Omar some work in your garage for a few weeks, yaar? The bugger's your nephew after all.

NASSER: (*VO on phone*) Why do you want to punish me?

INT. PAPA'S ROOM. DAY

PAPA *is speaking to* NASSER *on the phone. He watches* OMAR *slowly stirring dall in the kitchen.* OMAR *is, of course, listening.*

PAPA: He's on dole like everyone else in England. What's he doing home? Just roaming and moaning.

NASSER: (*VO on phone*) Haven't you trained him up to look after you, like I have with my girls?

PAPA: He brushes the dust from one place to another. He squeezes shirts and heats soup. But that hardly stretches him. Though his food stretches me. It's only for a few months, yaar. I'll send him to college in the autumn.

NASSER: (*VO*) He failed once. He had this chronic laziness that runs in our family except for me.

PAPA: If his arse gets lazy – kick it. I'll send a certificate giving permission. And one thing more. Try and fix him with a nice girl. I'm not sure if his penis is in full working order.

INT. FLAT. DAY

Later. OMAR *puts a full bottle of vodka on the table next to Papa's bed.*

PAPA: Go to your uncle's garage.

(*And* PAPA *pours himself a vodka.* OMAR *quickly thrusts a bottle of tomato juice towards* PAPA, *which* PAPA *ignores. Before* PAPA *can take a swig of the straight vodka,* OMAR *grabs the glass and adds tomato juice.* PAPA *takes it.*)

If Nasser wants to kick you – let him. I've given permission in two languages. (*To the photograph.*) The bloody's doing me a lot of good. Eh, bloody Mary?

EXT. STREET. DAY

OMAR *walks along a South London street, towards* NASSER's *garage. It's a rough area, beautiful in its own falling-down way.*

A youngish white BUSKER *is lying stoned in the doorway of a boarded-up shop, his guitar next to him.* OMAR *looks at him.*

Walking towards OMAR *from an amusement arcade across the street are* JOHNNY *and* GENGHIS *and* MOOSE. GENGHIS *is a well-built white man carrying a pile of right-wing newspapers, badges etc.* MOOSE *is a big white man,* GENGHIS's *lieutenant.*

JOHNNY *is an attractive man in his early twenties, quick and funny.*

OMAR *doesn't see* JOHNNY *but* JOHNNY *sees him and is startled. To avoid* OMAR, *in the middle of the road,* JOHNNY *takes* GENGHIS's *arm a moment.*

GENGHIS *stops suddenly.* MOOSE *charges into the back of him.* GENGHIS *drops the newspapers.* GENGHIS *remonstrates with* MOOSE. JOHNNY *watches* OMAR *go. The traffic stops while* MOOSE *picks up the newspapers.* GENGHIS *starts to sneeze.* MOOSE *gives him a handkerchief.*

They walk across the road, laughing at the waiting traffic.

They know the collapsed BUSKER. *He could even be a member of the gang.* JOHNNY *still watches* OMAR's *disappearing back.*

GENGHIS *and* MOOSE *prepare the newspapers.*

JOHNNY: (*Indicating* OMAR) That kid. We were like that.

GENGHIS: (*Sneezing over* MOOSE's *face*) You don't believe in nothing.

INT. UNDERGROUND GARAGE. DAY

Uncle Nasser's garage. It's a small private place where wealthy businessmen keep their cars during the day. It's almost full and contains about fifty cars – all Volvos, Rolls-Royces, Mercedes, Rovers, etc.

At the end of the garage is a small glassed-in office.

OMAR *is walking down the ramp and into the garage.*

INT. GARAGE OFFICE. DAY

The glassed-in office contains a desk, a filing cabinet, a typewriter, phone etc. With NASSER *is* SALIM.

SALIM *is a Pakistani in his late thirties, well-dressed in an expensive, smooth and slightly vulgar way. He moves restlessly about the office. Then he notices* OMAR *wandering about the garage. He watches him.*

Meanwhile, NASSER *is speaking on the phone in the background.*

NASSER: (*Into phone*) We've got one parking space, yes. It's £25 a week. And from this afternoon we provide a special on the premises 'clean-the-car' service. New thing.

(*From Salim's POV in the office, through the glass, we see* OMAR *trying the door of one of the cars.* SALIM *goes quickly out of the office.*)

INT. GARAGE. DAY

SALIM *stands outside the office and shouts at* OMAR. *The sudden sharp voice in the echoing garage.*

SALIM: Hey! Is that your car? Why are you feeling it up then? (OMAR *looks at him.*) Come here. Here, I said.

INT. GARAGE OFFICE. DAY

NASSER *puts down the phone.*

INT. GARAGE OFFICE. DAY

NASSER *is embracing* OMAR *vigorously, squashing him to him and bashing him lovingly on the back.*

NASSER: (*Introducing him to* SALIM.) This one who nearly beat you up is Salim. You'll see a lot of him.

SALIM: (*Shaking hands with* OMAR) I've heard many great things about your father.

NASSER: (*To* OMAR) I must see him. Oh God, how have I got time to do anything?

SALIM: You're too busy keeping this damn country in the black.

14

Someone's got to do it.

NASSER: (*To* OMAR) Your papa, he got thrown out of that
clerk's job I fixed him with? He was pissed?
(OMAR *nods.* NASSER *looks regretfully at the boy.*)
Can you wash a car?
(OMAR *looks uncertain.*)

SALIM: Have you washed a car before?
(OMAR *nods.*)
Your uncle can't pay you much. But you'll be able to
afford a decent shirt and you'll be with your own people.
Not in a dole queue. Mrs Thatcher will be pleased with
me.

INT. GARAGE. DAY

SALIM *and* OMAR *walk across the garage towards a big car.* OMAR
carries a full bucket of water and a cloth. He listens to SALIM.

SALIM: It's easy to wash a car. You just wet a rag and rub. You
know how to rub, don't you?
(*The bucket is overfull.* OMAR *carelessly bangs it against his leg.
Water slops out.* SALIM *dances away irritably.* OMAR *walks on.*
SALIM *points to a car.* RACHEL *swings down the ramp and into
the garage, gloriously.*)
Hi, baby.

RACHEL: My love.
(*And she goes into the garage office. We see her talking and
laughing with* NASSER.)

SALIM: (*Indicating car*) And you do this one first. Carefully, as if
you were restoring a Renaissance painting. It's my car.
(OMAR *looks up and watches as* RACHEL *and* NASSER *go out
through the back of the garage office into the room at the back.*)

INT. ROOM AT BACK OF GARAGE OFFICE. DAY

RACHEL *and* NASSER, *half-undressed, are drinking, laughing and
screwing on a bulging sofa in the wrecked room behind the office, no
bigger than a large cupboard.* RACHEL *is bouncing up and down on
his huge stomach in her red corset and outrageous worn-for-a-joke
underwear.*

NASSER: Rachel, fill my glass, darling.
(RACHEL *does so, then she begins to move on him.*)

RACHEL: Fill mine.

NASSER: What am I, Rachel, your trampoline?

RACHEL: Yes, oh, je vous aime beaucoup, trampoline.

NASSER: Speak my language, dammit.

RACHEL: I do nothing else. Nasser, d'you think we'll ever part?

NASSER: Not at the moment.
    (*Slapping her arse*) Keep moving, I love you. You move . . .
    Christ . . . like a liner . . .

RACHEL: And can't we go away somewhere?

NASSER: Yes, I'm taking you.

RACHEL: Where?

NASSER: Kempton Park, Saturday.

RACHEL: Great. We'll take the boy.

NASSER: No, I've got big plans for him.

RACHEL: You're going to make him work?

INT. GARAGE OFFICE. DAY

OMAR *has come into the garage office with his car-washing bucket
and sponge.* SALIM *has gone home.* OMAR *is listening at the door to
his uncle* NASSER *and* RACHEL *screwing. He hears:*

NASSER: Work? That boy? You'll think the word was invented
    for him!

INT. COCKTAIL BAR/CLUB. EVENING

RACHEL *and* NASSER *have taken* OMAR *to Anwar's club/bar.*
OMAR *watches Anwar's son* TARIQ *behind the bar.* TARIQ *is rather
contemptuous of* OMAR *and listens to their conversation.*

    OMAR *eats peanuts and olives off the bar.* TARIQ *removes the
bowl.*

NASSER: By the way, Rachel is my old friend. (*To her.*) Eh?

OMAR: (*To* NASSER) How's Auntie Bilquis?

NASSER: (*Glancing at amused* RACHEL) She's at home with the
    kids.

OMAR: Papa sends his love. Uncle, if I picked Papa up–

NASSER: (*Indicating the club*) Have you been to a high-class
    place like this before? I suppose you stay in that black-hole
    flat all the time.

OMAR: If I picked Papa up, uncle –

NASSER: (*To* RACHEL) He's one of those underprivileged types.

OMAR: And squeezed him, squeezed Papa out, like that, Uncle, I often imagine. I'd get –

NASSER: Two fat slaps.

OMAR: Two bottles of pure vodka. And a kind of flap of skin. (*To* RACHEL.) Like a French letter.

NASSER: What are you talking, madman? I love my brother. And I love you.

OMAR: I don't understand how you can . . . love me.

NASSER: Because you're such a prick?

OMAR: You can't be sure that I am.

RACHEL: Nasser.

NASSER: She's right. Don't deliberately egg me on to laugh at you when I've brought you here to tell you one essential thing. Move closer.
(OMAR *attempts to drag the stool he is sitting on near to* NASSER. *He crashes off it.* RACHEL *helps him up, laughing.* TARIQ *also laughs.* NASSER *is solicitous.*)
In this damn country which we hate and love, you can get anything you want. It's all spread out and available. That's why I believe in England. You just have to know how to squeeze the tits of the system.

RACHEL: (*To* OMAR) He's saying he wants to help you.

OMAR: What are you going to do with me?

NASSER: What am I going to do with you? Make you into something damn good. Your father can't now, can he?
(RACHEL *nods at* NASSER *and he takes out his wallet. He gives* OMAR *money.* OMAR *doesn't want to take it.* NASSER *shoves it down Omar's jumper, then cuddles his confused nephew.*)
Damn fool, you're just like a son to me. (*Looking at* RACHEL.) To both of us.

INT. GARAGE. DAY
OMAR *is vigorously washing down a car, the last to be cleaned in the garage. The others cars are gleaming.* NASSER *comes quickly out of the office and watches* OMAR *squeezing a cloth over a bucket.*

NASSER: You like this work? (OMAR *shrugs.*) Come on, for Christ's sake, take a look at these accounts for me.
(OMAR *follows him into the garage office.*)

17

INT. GARAGE OFFICE. NIGHT

OMAR *is sitting at the office desk in his shirt-sleeves. The desk is covered with papers. He's been sitting there some time and it is late. Most of the cars in the garage have gone.*

NASSER *drives into the garage, wearing evening clothes.* RACHEL, *looking divine, is with him.* OMAR *goes out to them.*

INT. GARAGE. NIGHT

NASSER: (*From the car*) Kiss Rachel. (OMAR *kisses her.*)

OMAR: I'll finish the paperwork tonight, Uncle.

NASSER: (*To* RACHEL) He's such a good worker I'm going to promote him.

RACHEL: What to?

NASSER: (*To* OMAR) Come to my house next week and I'll tell you.

RACHEL: It's far. How will he get there?

NASSER: I'll give him a car, dammit. (*He points to an old convertible parked in the garage. It has always looked out of place.*) The keys are in the office. Anything he wants. (*He moves the car off. To* OMAR.) Oh yes, I've got a real challenge lined up for you.

(RACHEL *blows him a kiss as they drive off.*)

INT. PAPA'S FLAT. EVENING

PAPA *is lying on the bed drinking.* OMAR, *in new clothes, tie undone, comes into the room and puts a plate of steaming food next to* PAPA. *Stew and potatoes.* OMAR *turns away and looking in the mirror snips at the hair in his nostrils with a large pair of scissors.*

PAPA: You must be getting married. Why else would you be dressed like an undertaker on holiday?

OMAR: Going to Uncle's house, Papa. He's given me a car.

PAPA: What? The brakes must be faulty. Tell me one thing because there's something I don't understand, though it must be my fault. How is it that scrubbing cars can make a son of mine look so ecstatic?

OMAR: It gets me out of the house.

PAPA: Don't get too involved with that crook. You've got to study. We are under siege by the white man. For us education is power.

(OMAR *shakes his head at his father.*)
Don't let me down.

EXT. COUNTRY LANE. EVENING
OMAR, *in the old convertible, speeds along a country lane in Kent.
The car has its roof down, although it's raining. Loud music playing
on the radio.*
*He turns into the drive of a large detached house. The house is
brightly lit. There are seven or eight cars in the drive.* OMAR *sits there
a moment, music blaring.*

INT. LIVING ROOM IN NASSER'S HOUSE. EVENING
A large living room furnished in the modern style. A shy OMAR *has
been led in by* BILQUIS, *Nasser's wife. She is a shy, middle-aged
Pakistani woman. She speaks and understands English, but is
uncertain in the language. But she is warm and friendly.*
OMAR *has already been introduced to most of the women in the
room.*
*There are five women there: a selection of wives; plus Bilquis's
three daughters. The eldest,* TANIA, *is in her early twenties.*
CHERRY, *Salim's Anglo-Indian wife is there.*
*Some of the women are wearing saris or salwar kamiz, though not
necessarily only the Pakistani women.*
TANIA *wears jeans and T-shirt. She watches* OMAR *all through
this and* OMAR, *when he can, glances at her. She is attracted to him.*
BILQUIS: (*To* OMAR) and this is Salim's wife, Cherry. And of
course you remember our three naughty daughters.
CHERRY: (*Ebulliently to* BILQUIS) He has his family's
cheekbones, Bilquis. (*To* OMAR.) I know all your gorgeous
family in Karachi.
OMAR: (*This is a faux pas*) You've been there?
CHERRY: You stupid, what a stupid, it's my home. Could
anyone in their right mind call this silly little island off
Europe their home? Every day in Karachi, every day your
other uncles and cousins are at our house for bridge, booze
and VCR.
BILQUIS: Cherry, my little nephew knows nothing of that life
there.
CHERRY: Oh God, I'm so sick of hearing about these

in-betweens. People should make up their minds where
they are.

TANIA: Uncle's next door. (*Leading him away. Quietly.*) Can
you see me later? I'm so bored with these people.

(CHERRY *stares at* TANIA, *not approving of this whispering
and cousin-closeness.* TANIA *glares back defiantly at her.*
BILQUIS *looks warmly at* OMAR.)

INT. CORRIDOR OF NASSER'S HOUSE. DAY
TANIA *takes* OMAR *by the hand down the corridor to Nasser's room.
She opens the door and leads him in.*

INT. NASSER'S ROOM. EVENING
*Nasser's room is further down the corridor. It's his bedroom but
where he receives guests. And he has a VCR in the room, a fridge,
small bar, etc. Behind his bed a window which overlooks the garden.*
    OMAR *goes into the smoke-filled room, led by* TANIA. *She goes.*
    NASSER *is lying on his bed in the middle of the room like a fat
king. His cronies are gathered round the bed.* ZAKI, SALIM, *an*
ENGLISHMAN *and an American called* DICK O'DONNELL.
    They're shouting and hooting and boozing and listening to
NASSER's *story, which he tells with great energy.* OMAR *stands inside
the door shyly, and takes in the scene.*

NASSER: There'd been some tappings on the window. But who
would stay in a hotel without tappings? My brother
Hussein, the boy's papa, in his usual way hadn't turned up
and I was asleep. I presumed he was screwing some
barmaid somewhere. Then when these tappings went on I
got out of bed and opened the door to the balcony. and
there he was, standing outside. With some woman! They
were completely without clothes! And blue with cold! They
looked like two bars of soap. This I refer to as my brother's
blue period.

DICK O'DONNELL: What happened to the woman?

NASSER: He married her.

(*When* NASSER *notices the boy, conversation ceases with a
wave of his hand. And* NASSER *unembarrassedly calls him over
to be fondled and patted.*) Come along, come along. Your
father's a good man.

DICK O'DONNELL: This is the famous Hussein's son?

NASSER: The exact bastard. My blue brother was also a famous journalist in Bombay and great drinker. He was to the bottle what Louis Armstrong is to the trumpet.

SALIM: But you are to the bookie what Mother Theresa is to the children.

ZAKI: (*To* NASSER) Your brother was the clever one. You used to carry his typewriter.

(TANIA *appears at the window behind the bed, where no one sees her but* OMAR *and then* ZAKI. *Later in the scene, laughing and to distract the serious-faced* OMAR, *she bares her breasts.* ZAKI *sees this and cannot believe his swimming-in-drink eyes.*)

DICK O'DONNELL: Isn't he coming tonight?

SALIM (*To* NASSER) Whatever happened to him?

OMAR: Papa's lying down.

SALIM: I meant his career.

NASSER: That's lying down too. What chance would the Englishman give a leftist communist Pakistani on newspapers?

OMAR: Socialist. Socialist.

NASSER: What chance would the Englishman give a leftist communist socialist?

ZAKI: What chance has the racist Englishman given us that we haven't torn from him with our hands? Let's face up to it.

(*And* ZAKI *has seen the breasts of* TANIA. *He goes white and panics.*)

NASSER: Zaki, have another stiff drink for that good point!

ZAKI: Nasser, please God, I am on the verge already!

ENGLISHMAN: Maybe Omar's father didn't make chances for himself. Look at you, Salim, five times richer and more powerful than me.

SALIM: Five times? Ten, at least.

ENGLISHMAN: In my country! The only prejudice in England is against the useless.

SALIM: It's rather tilted in favour of the useless I would think. The only positive discrimination they have here.

(*The* PAKISTANIS *in the room laugh at this. The* ENGLISHMAN *looks annoyed.* DICK O'DONNELL *smiles sympathetically at the* ENGLISHMAN.)

DICK O'DONNELL: (*To* NASSER) Can I make this nice boy a drink?

NASSER: Make him a man first.

SALIM: (*To* ZAKI) Give him a drink. I like him. He's our future.

INT. THE VERANDAH. NIGHT

OMAR *shuts the door of Nasser's room and walks down the hall, to a games room at the end. This is a verandah overlooking the garden. There's a table-tennis table, various kids' toys, an exercise cycle, some cane chairs and on the walls numerous photographs of India.*

   TANIA *turns as he enters and goes eagerly to him, touching him warmly.*

TANIA: It's been years. And you're looking good now. I bet we understand each other, eh?

   (*He can't easily respond to her enthusiasm. Unoffended, she swings away from him. He looks at photographs of his Papa and Bhutto on the wall.*)

   Are they being cruel to you in their typical men's way? (*He shrugs.*) You don't mind?

OMAR: I think I should harden myself.

TANIA: (*Patting seat next to her*) Wow, what are you into?

OMAR: Your father's done well.

   (*He sits. She kisses him on the lips. They hold each other.*)

TANIA: Has he? He adores you. I expect he wants you to take over the businesses. He wouldn't think of asking me. But he is too vicious to people in his work. He doesn't want you to work in that shitty laundrette, does he?

OMAR: What's wrong with it?

TANIA: And he has a mistress, doesn't he?

   (OMAR *looks up and sees* AUNTI BILQUIS *standing at the door.* TANIA *doesn't see her.*)

   Rachel. Yes, I can tell from your face. Does he love her? Yes. Families, I hate families.

BILQUIS: Please Tania, can you come and help.

   (BILQUIS *goes.* TANIA *follows her.*)

INT. HALL OF NASSER'S HOUSE. DAY

OMAR *is standing in the hall of Nasser's house as the guests leave their respective rooms and go out into the drive.* OMAR *stands there.*

NASSER *shouts to him from his bed.*

NASSER: Take my advice. There's money in muck.

(TANIA *signals and shakes her head.*)

What is it the gora Englishman always needs? Clean clothes!

EXT. NASSER'S DRIVE. NIGHT

OMAR *has come out of the house and into the drive. A strange sight:* SALIM *staggering about drunkenly. The* ENGLISHMAN, ZAKI *and* CHERRY *try to get him into the car.* SALIM *screams at* ZAKI.

SALIM: Don't you owe me money? Why not? You usually owe me money! Here, take this! Borrow it! (*And he starts to scatter money about.*) Pick it up!

(ZAKI *starts picking it up. He is afraid.*)

CHERRY: (*To* OMAR) Drive us back, will you. Pick up your own car tomorrow. Salim is not feeling well.

(*As* ZAKI *bends over,* SALIM *who is laughing, goes to kick him.* BILQUIS *stands at the window watching all this.*)

INT. SALIM'S CAR, DRIVING INTO SOUTH LONDON. NIGHT

OMAR *driving* SALIM*'s car enthusiastically into London.* CHERRY *and* SALIM *are in the back. The car comes to a stop at traffic lights.*

On the adjacent pavement outside a chip shop a group of LADS *are kicking cans about. The* LADS *include* MOOSE *and* GENGHIS.

A lively street of the illuminated shops, amusement arcades and late-night shops of South London.

MOOSE *notices that Pakistanis are in the car. And he indicates to the others.*

The LADS *gather round the car and bang on it and shout. From inside the car this noise is terrifying.* CHERRY *starts to scream.*

SALIM: Drive, you bloody fool, drive!

(*But* MOOSE *climbs on the bonnet of the car and squashes his arse grotesquely against the windscreen. Faces squash against the other windows.*

Looking out of the side window OMAR *sees* JOHNNY *standing to one side of the car, not really part of the car-climbing and banging.*

Impulsively, unafraid, OMAR *gets out of the car.*)

EXT. STREET. NIGHT

OMAR *walks past* GENGHIS *and* MOOSE *and the others to the embarrassed* JOHNNY. CHERRY *is yelling after him from inside the open-doored car.*

The LADS *are alert and ready for violence but are confused by* OMAR*'s obvious friendship with* JOHNNY.

OMAR *sticks out his hand and* JOHNNY *takes it.*

OMAR: It's me.

JOHNNY: I know who it is.

OMAR: How are yer? Working? What you doing now then?

JOHNNY: Oh, this kinda thing.

CHERRY: (*Yelling from the car*) Come on, come on!
    (*The lads laugh at her.* SALIM *is hastily giving* MOOSE *cigarettes.*)

JOHNNY: What are you now, chauffeur?

OMAR: No. I'm on to something.

JOHNNY: What?

OMAR: I'll let you know. Still living in the same place?

JOHNNY: Na, don't get on with me mum and dad. You?

OMAR: She died last year, my mother. Jumped on to the railway line.

JOHNNY: Yeah. I heard. All the trains stopped.

OMAR: I'm still there. Got the number?

JOHNNY: (*Indicates the* LADS) Like me friends?
    (CHERRY *starts honking the car horn. The* LADS *cheer.*)

OMAR: Ring us then.

JOHNNY: I will. (*Indicates car.*) Leave 'em there. We can do something. Now. Just us.

OMAR: Can't.
    (OMAR *touches* JOHNNY*'s arm and runs back to the car.*)

INT. CAR. NIGHT

They continue to drive. CHERRY *is screaming at* OMAR.

CHERRY: What the hell were you doing?
    (SALIM *slaps her.*)

SALIM: He saved our bloody arses! (*To* OMAR, *grabbing him round the neck and pressing his face close to his.*) I'm going to see you're all right!

INT. PAPA'S ROOM. NIGHT

OMAR *has got home. He creeps into the flat. He goes carefully along the hall, fingertips on familiar wall.*

He goes into Papa's room. No sign of PAPA. PAPA *is on the balcony. Just a shadow.*

EXT. BALCONY. NIGHT

PAPA *is swaying on the balcony like a little tree. Papa's pyjama bottoms have fallen down. And he's just about maintaining himself vertically. His hair has fallen across his terrible face. A train bangs towards him, rushing out of the darkness. And* PAPA *sways precariously towards it.*

OMAR: (*Screams above the noise*) What are you doing?

PAPA: I want to pee.

OMAR: Can't you wait for me to take you?

PAPA: My prick will drop off before you show up these days.

OMAR: (*Pulling up Papa's bottoms*) You know who I met? Johnny. Johnny.

PAPA: The boy who came here one day dressed as a fascist with a quarter inch of hair?

OMAR: He was a friend once. For years.

PAPA: There were days when he didn't deserve your admiration so much.

OMAR: Christ, I've known him since I was five.

PAPA: He went too far. They hate us in England. And all you do is kiss their arses and think of yourself as a little Britisher!

INT. PAPA'S ROOM. NIGHT

They are inside the room now, and OMAR *shuts the doors.*

OMAR: I'm being promoted. To Uncle's laundrette.

(PAPA *pulls a pair of socks from his pyjama pockets and thrusts them at* OMAR.)

PAPA: Illustrate your washing methods!

(OMAR *throws the socks across the room.*)

EXT. SOUTH LONDON STREET. DAY

NASSER *and* OMAR *get out of Nasser's car and walk over the road to the laundrette. It's called 'Churchills'. It's broad and spacious and in*

*bad condition. It's situated in an area of run-down second-hand
shops, betting shops, grocers with their windows boarded-up, etc.*

NASSER: It's nothing but a toilet and a youth club now. A finger
up my damn arse.

INT. LAUNDRETTE. DAY
*We are inside the laundrette. Some of the benches in the laundrette
are church pews.*

OMAR: Where did you get those?

NASSER: Church.

> (*Three or four rough-lookings* KIDS, *boys and girls, one of
> whom isn't wearing shoes, sitting on the pews. A character by
> the telephone. The thunderous sound of running-shoes in a spin-
> drier. The* KID *coolly opens the spin-drier and takes out his
> shoes.*)

Punkey, that's how machines get buggered!

> (*The* KID *puts on his shoes. He offers his hot-dog to another*
> KID, *who declines it. So the* KID *flings it into a spin-drier.*
>   NASSER *moves to throttle him. He gets the* KID *by the throat.
> The other* KIDS *get up.* OMAR *pulls his eager* UNCLE *away.
> The* TELEPHONE CHARACTER *looks suspiciously at everyone.
> Then makes his call.*)

TELEPHONE CHARACTER: Hi, baby, it's number one here, baby.
How's your foot now?

INT. BACK ROOM OF LAUNDRETTE. DAY
NASSER *stands at the desk going through bills and papers.*

NASSER: (*To* OMAR) Get started. There's the broom. Move it!

OMAR: I don't only want to sweep up.

NASSER: What are you now, Labour Party?

OMAR: I want to be manager of this place. I think I can do it.
(*Pause.*) Please let me.
(NASSER *thinks.*)

NASSER: I'm just thinking how to tell your father that four
punks drowned you in a washing machine. On the other
hand, some water on the brain might clear your thoughts.
Okay. Pay me a basic rent. Above that – you keep.
(*He goes quickly, eager to get out. The* TELEPHONE
CHARACTER *is shouting into the phone.*)

TELEPHONE CHARACTER: (*Into phone*) Was it my fault? But you're everything to me! More than everything. I prefer you to Janice!
(*The* TELEPHONE CHARACTER *indicates to* NASSER *that a washing machine has overflowed all over the floor, with soap suds.* NASSER *gets out.* OMAR *looks on.*)

INT. BACK ROOM OF LAUNDRETTE. DAY
OMAR *sitting gloomily in the back room. The door to the main area open.* KIDS *push each other about. Straight customers are intimidated.*
   From Omar's POV through the laundrette windows, we see
SALIM *getting out of his car.* SALIM *walks in through the laundrette, quickly. Comes into the back room, slamming the door behind him.*
SALIM: Get up! (OMAR *gets up.* SALIM *rams the back of a chair under the door handle.*) I've had trouble here.
OMAR: Salim, please. I don't know how to make this place work. I'm afraid I've made a fool of myself.
SALIM: You'll never make a penny out of this. Your uncle's given you a dead duck. That's why I've decided to help you financially. (*He gives him a piece of paper with an address on it. He also gives him money.*) Go to this house near the airport. Pick up some video cassettes and bring them to my flat. That's all.

INT. SALIM'S FLAT. EVENING
The flat is large and beautiful. Some Sindi music playing. SALIM *comes out of the bathroom wearing only a towel round his waist. And a plastic shower cap. He is smoking a fat joint.*
   CHERRY *goes into another room.*
   OMAR *stands there with the cassettes in his arms.* SALIM *indicates them.*
SALIM: Put them. Relax. No problems? (SALIM *gives him the joint and* OMAR *takes a hit on it.* SALIM *points at the walls. Some erotic and some very good paintings.*) One of the best collections of recent Indian painting. I patronize many painters. I won't be a minute. Watch something if you like. (SALIM *goes back into the bedroom.* OMAR *puts one of the cassettes he has brought into the VCR. But there's nothing on*

the tape. Just a screenful of static.

Meanwhile, OMAR *makes a call, taking the number off a piece of paper.*)

OMAR: (*Into phone*) Can I speak to Johnny? D'you know where he's staying? Are you sure? Just wanted to help him. Please, if you see him, tell him to ring Omo.

INT. SALIM'S FLAT. EVENING

Dressed now, and ready to go out, SALIM *comes quickly into the room. He picks up the video cassettes and realizes one is being played.* SALIM *screams savagely at* OMAR.

SALIM: Is that tape playing? (OMAR *nods.*) What the hell are you doing? (*He pulls the tape out of the VCR and examines it.*)

OMAR: Just watching something, Salim.

SALIM: Not these! Who gave you permission to touch these?

(OMAR *grabs the tape from* SALIM'*s hand.*)

OMAR: It's just a tape!

SALIM: Not to me!

OMAR: What are you doing? What business, Salim?

(SALIM *pushes* OMAR *hard and* OMAR *crashes backwards across the room. As he gets up quickly to react* SALIM *is at him, shoving him back down, viciously. He puts his foot on* OMAR'*s nose.*

CHERRY *watches him coolly, leaning against a door jamb.*)

SALIM: Nasser tells me you're ambitious to do something. But twice you failed your exams. You've done nothing with the laundrette and now you bugger me up. You've got too much white blood. It's made you weak like those pale-faced adolescents that call us wog. You know what I do to them? I take out this. (*He takes out a pound note. He tears it to pieces.*) I say: your English pound is worthless. It's worthless like you, Omar, are worthless. Your whole great family – rich and powerful over there – is let down by you. (OMAR *gets up slowly.*)

Now fuck off.

OMAR: I'll do something to you for this.

SALIM: I'd be truly happy to see you try.

EXT. OUTSIDE LAUNDRETTE. EVENING

OMAR, *depressed after his humiliation at* SALIM*'s, drives slowly past the laundrette. Music plays over this. It's raining and the laundrette looks grim and hopeless.*

OMAR *sees* GENGHIS *and* MOOSE. *He drives up alongside them.*

OMAR: Seen Johnny?

GENGHIS: Get back to the jungle, wog boy.

(MOOSE *kicks the side of the car.*)

INT. PAPA'S ROOM. EVENING

OMAR *is cutting* PAPA*'s long toenails with a large pair of scissors.* OMAR*'s face is badly bruised.* PAPA *jerks about, pouring himself a drink. So* OMAR *has to keep grabbing at his feet. The skin on* PAPA*'s legs is peeling through lack of vitamins.*

PAPA: Those people are too tough for you. I'll tell Nasser
    you're through with them. (PAPA *dials. We hear it ringing in
    Nasser's house. He puts the receiver to one side to pick up his
    drink. He looks at* OMAR *who wells with anger and
    humiliation.* TANIA *answers.*)

TANIA: Hallo.

(OMAR *moves quickly and breaks the connection.*)

PAPA: (*Furious*) Why do that, you useless fool?

    (OMAR *grabs* PAPA*'s foot and starts on the toe job again. The
    phone starts to ring.* PAPA *pulls away and* OMAR *jabs him with
    the scissors. And* PAPA *bleeds.* OMAR *answers the phone.*)

OMAR: Hallo. (*Pause.*) Johnny.

PAPA: (*Shouts over*) I'll throw you out of this bloody flat, you're
    nothing but a bum liability!

    (*But* OMAR *is smiling into the phone and talking to* JOHNNY, *a
    finger in one ear.*)

INT. THE LAUNDRETTE. DAY

OMAR *is showing* JOHNNY *round the laundrette.*

JOHNNY: I'm dead impressed by all this.

OMAR: You were the one at school. The one they liked.

JOHNNY: (*Sarcastic*) All the Pakis liked me.

OMAR: I've been through it. With my parents and that. And
    with people like you. But now there's some things I want
    to do. Some pretty big things I've got in mind. I need to

raise money to make this place good. I want you to help
me do that. And I want you to work here with me.

JOHNNY: What kinda work is it?

OMAR: Variety. Variety of menial things.

JOHNNY: Cleaning windows kinda thing, yeah?

OMAR: Yeah. Sure. And clean out those bastards, will ya?

(OMAR *indicates the sitting* KIDS *playing about on the benches.*)

JOHNNY: Now?

OMAR: I'll want everything done now. That's the only attitude if
you want to do anything big.

(JOHNNY *goes to the* KIDS *and stands above them. Slowly he
removes his watch and puts it in his pocket. This is a strangely
threatening gesture. The* KIDS *rise and walk out one by one.
One* KID *resents this. He pushes* JOHNNY *suddenly.* JOHNNY
kicks him hard.)

EXT. OUTSIDE THE LAUNDRETTE. DAY

Continuous. The kicked KID *shoots across the pavement and crashes
into* SALIM *who is getting out of his car.* SALIM *pushes away the
frantic arms and legs and goes quickly into the laundrette.*

INT. LAUNDRETTE. DAY

SALIM *drags the reluctant* OMAR *by the arm into the back room of
the laundrette.* JOHNNY *watches them, then follows.*

INT. BACK ROOM OF LAUNDRETTE. DAY

SALIM *lets go of* OMAR *and grabs a chair to stuff under the door
handle as before.* OMAR *suddenly snatches the chair from him and
puts it down slowly. And* JOHNNY, *taking* OMAR'S *lead, sticks his
big boot in the door as* SALIM *attempts to slam it.*

SALIM: Christ, Omar, sorry what happened before. Too much
to drink. Just go on one little errand for me, eh? (*He opens*
OMAR'*s fingers and presses a piece of paper into his hand.*) Like
before. For me.

OMAR: For fifty quid as well.

SALIM: You little bastard.

(OMAR *turns away.* JOHNNY *turns away too, mocking* SALIM,
parodying OMAR.)

All right.

INT. HOTEL ROOM. DUSK

OMAR *is standing in a hotel room. A modern high building with a view over London. He is with a middle-aged Pakistani who is wearing salwar kamiz. Suitcases on the floor.*

The MAN *has a long white beard. Suddenly he peels if off and hands it to* OMAR. OMAR *is astonished. The* MAN *laughs uproariously.*

INT. LAUNDRETTE. EVENNG

JOHNNY *is doing a service wash in the laundrette.* OMAR *comes in quickly, the beard in a plastic bag. He puts the beard on.*

JOHNNY: You fool.

(OMAR *pulls* JOHNNY *towards the back room.*)

OMAR: I've sussed Salim's game. This is going to finance our whole future.

INT. BACK ROOM OF LAUNDRETTE. DAY

JOHNNY *and* OMAR *sitting at the desk.* JOHNNY *is unpicking the back of the beard with a pair of scissors. The door to the laundrette is closed.*

JOHNNY *carefully pulls plastic bags out of the back of the beard. He looks enquiringly at* OMAR. OMAR *confidently indicates that he should open one of them.* OMAR *looks doubtfully at him.* OMAR *pulls the chair closer.* JOHNNY *snips a corner off the bag. He opens it and tastes the powder on his finger. He nods at* OMAR. JOHNNY *quickly starts stuffing the bags back in the beard.*

OMAR *gets up.*

OMAR: Take them out. You know where to sell this stuff. Yes? Don't you?

JOHNNY: I wouldn't be working for you now if I wanted to go on being a bad boy.

OMAR: This means more. Real work. Expansion.

(JOHNNY *reluctantly removes the rest of the packets from the back of the beard.*)

We'll re-sell it fast. Tonight.

JOHNNY: Salim'll kill us.

OMAR: Why should he find out it's us? Better get this back to him. Come on. I couldn't be doing any of this without you.

INT. OUTSIDE SALIM'S FLAT. NIGHT
OMAR, *wearing the beard, is standing outside* SALIM*'s flat, having rung the bell.* CHERRY *answers the door. At first she doesn't recognize him. Then he laughs. And she pulls him in.*

INT. SALIM'S FLAT. NIGHT
There are ten people sitting in SALIM*'s flat. Well-off Pakistani friends who have come round for dinner. They are chatting and drinking. At the other end of the room the table has been laid for dinner.*

 SALIM *is fixing drinks, and talking to his friends over his shoulder.*
SALIM: We were all there, yaar, to see Ravi Shankar. But you all just wanted to talk about my paintings. My collection. That's why I said, why don't you all come round. I will turn my place into an art gallery for the evening . . . (*The friends are giggling at* OMAR, *who is wearing the beard.* SALIM, *disturbed, turns suddenly.* SALIM *is appalled by* OMAR *in the beard.*) Let's have a little private chat, eh?

INT. SALIM'S BEDROOM. EVENING
SALIM *snatches the beard from* OMAR*'s chin. He goes into the bathroom with it.* OMAR *moves towards the bathroom and watches* SALIM *frantically examine the back of the beard. When* SALIM *sees, in the mirror,* OMAR *watching him, he kicks the door shut.*

INT. SALIM'S BEDROOM. NIGHT
SALIM *comes back into the bedroom from the bathroom. He throws down the beard.*
SALIM: You can go.
OMAR: But you haven't paid me.
SALIM: I'm not in the mood. Nothing happened to you on the way here? (OMAR *shakes his head.*) Well, something may happen to you on the way back. (SALIM *is unsure at the moment what's happened.* OMAR *watches him steadily. His nerve is holding out.*) Get the hell out.

EXT. OUTSIDE SALIM'S FLAT. NIGHT
As OMAR *runs down the steps of the flats to* JOHNNY *waiting in the revving car,* SALIM *stands at the window of his flat, watching them. Music over. We go with the music into:*

INT. CLUB/BAR. NIGHT
OMAR *has taken* JOHNNY *to the club he visited with* NASSER *and* RACHEL.

The club is more lively in the evening, with West Indian, English and Pakistani customers. All affluent. In fact, a couple of the JAMAICANS *from the opening scene are there.*

OMAR *and* JOHNNY *are sitting at a table.* TARIQ, *the young son of the club's owner, stands beside them. He puts two menus down.*

TARIQ: (*To* OMAR) Of course a table is always here for you. Your Uncle Nasser – a great man. And Salim, of course. No one touches him. No one. You want to eat?

OMAR: Tariq, later. Bring us champagne first. (TARIQ *goes. To* JOHNNY.) Okay?

JOHNNY: I'm selling the stuff tonight. The bloke's coming here in an hour. He's testing it now.

OMAR: Good. (*Smiles at a girl.*) She's nice.

JOHNNY: Yes.

INT. CLUB/BAR. NIGHT
OMAR *is sitting alone at the table, drinking.* TARIQ *clears the table and goes.* JOHNNY *comes out of the toilet with the white* DEALER. *The* DEALER *goes.* JOHNNY *goes and sits beside* OMAR.

JOHNNY: We're laughing.

INT. NASSER'S ROOM. EVENING
NASSER *is lying on his bed wearing salwar kamiz. One of the young* DAUGHTERS *is pressing his legs and he groans with delight.* OMAR *is sitting across the room from him, well-dressed and relaxed. He eats Indian sweets. The other* DAUGHTER *comes in with more sweets, which she places by* OMAR.

OMAR: Tell me about the beach at Bombay, Uncle. Juhu beach.

(*But* NASSER *is in a bad mood.* TANIA *comes into the room. She is wearing salwar kamiz for the first time in the film. And she looks stunning. She has dressed up for* OMAR.)

(*Playing to* TANIA) Or the house in Lahore. When Auntie Nina put the garden hose in the window of my father's bedroom because he wouldn't get up. And Papa's bed started to float.

(TANIA *stands behind* OMAR *and touches him gently on the shoulder. She is laughing at the story.*)

TANIA: Papa.

(*But he ignores her.*)

OMAR: (*To* TANIA) You look beautiful.

(*She squeezes his arm.*)

NASSER: (*Sitting up suddenly*) What about my damn laundrette? Damn these stories about a place you've never been. What are you doing, boy!

OMAR: What am I doing?

INT. LAUNDRETTE. DAY

OMAR *and* JOHNNY *in the laundrette.* JOHNNY, *with an axe, is smashing one of the broken-down benches off the wall while* OMAR *stands there surveying the laundrette, pencil and pad in hand. Splinters, bits of wood fly about as* JOHNNY, *athletically and enthusiastically singing at the top of his voice, demolishes existing structures.*

OMAR: (*Voice over*) It'll be going into profit any day now. Partly because I've hired a bloke of outstanding competence and strength of body and mind to look after it with me.

INT. NASSER'S ROOM. EVENING

NASSER: (*To young* DAUGHTER) Jasmine, fiddle with my toes.
(*To* OMAR) What bloke?

INT. LAUNDRETTE. DAY

JOHNNY *is up a ladder vigorously painting a wall and singing loudly. The washing machines are covered with white sheets. Pots and paints and brushes lie about.*

OMAR *watches* JOHNNY.

OMAR: (*Voice over*) He's called Johnny.

NASSER: (*Voice over*) How will you pay him?

INT. NASSER'S ROOM. EVENING

SALIM *and* ZAKI *come into the room.* SALIM *carries a bottle of whisky.* ZAKI *looks nervously at* TANIA *who flutters her eyelashes at him.*

SALIM *and* ZAKI *shake hands with* NASSER *and sit down in chairs round the bed.*

ZAKI: (*To* NASSER) How are you, you old bastard?

NASSER: (*Pointing to drinks*) Tania.

(TANIA *fixes drinks for everyone.* SALIM *looks suspiciously at* OMAR *through this. But* OMAR *coolly ignores him.*)

Zaki, how's things now then?

ZAKI: Oh good, good, everything. But . . .

(*He begins to explain about his declining laundrette business and how bad his heart is, in Urdu.* NASSER *waves at* OMAR.)

NASSER: Speak in English, Zaki, so this boy can understand.

ZAKI: He doesn't understand his own language?

NASSER: (*With affectionate mock anger*) Not only that. I've given him that pain-in-the-arse laundrette to run.

SALIM: I know.

NASSER: But this is the point. He's hired someone else to do the work!

ZAKI: Typically English, if I can say that.

SALIM: (*Harshly*) Don't fuck your uncle's business, you little fool.

TANIA: I don't think you should talk to him like that, Uncle.

SALIM: Why, what is he, royalty?

(SALIM *and* NASSER *exchange amused looks.*)

ZAKI: (*To* NASSER) She is a hot girl.

TANIA: I don't like it.

OMAR: (*To* SALIM) In my small opinion, much good can come of fucking.

(TANIA *laughs.* ZAKI *is shocked.* SALIM *stares at* OMAR.)

NASSER: (*To* OMAR) Your mouth is getting very big lately.

OMAR: Well. (*And he gets up quickly, to walk out.*)

NASSER: All right, all right, let's all take it easy.

SALIM: Who is it sitting in the drive? It's bothering me.

(*To* TANIA.) Some friend of yours?

(*She shakes her head.*)

NASSER: Zaki, go and check it for me please.

OMAR: It's only Johnny. My friend. He works for me.

NASSER: No one works without my permission.

(*To* TANIA.) Bring him here now.

(*She goes.* OMAR *gets up and follows her.*)

EXT. NASSER'S FRONT DRIVE. EVENING

JOHNNY *is standing by the car, music coming from the car radio.*
TANIA *and* OMAR *walk over to him.* TANIA *takes* OMAR*'s arm.*

TANIA: I know why you put up with them. Because there's so much you want. You're greedy like my father. (*Nodding towards* JOHNNY.) Why did you leave him out here?

OMAR: He's lower class. He won't come in without being asked. Unless he's doing a burglary.

(*They get to* JOHNNY, OMAR *not minding if he overhears the last remark.*)

TANIA: Come in, Johnny. My father's waiting for you.

(*She turns and walks away.* OMAR *and* JOHNNY *walk towards the house.* BILQUIS *is standing in the window of the front room, looking at them.* OMAR *smiles and waves at her.*)

JOHNNY: How's Salim today?

OMAR: Wearing too much perfume as usual. (OMAR *stops* JOHNNY *a moment and brushes his face.*) An eyelash.

(TANIA, *waiting at the door, watches this piece of affection and wonders.*)

INT. NASSER'S ROOM, EVENING

NASSER, SALIM, JOHNNY, ZAKI *and* OMAR *are laughing together at one of Nasser's stories.* JOHNNY *has been introduced and they are getting along well.* TANIA *hands* SALIM *another drink and checks that everyone else has drinks.*

NASSER: . . . So I said, in my street I am the law! You see, I make wealth, I create money.

(*There is a slight pause.* NASSER *indicates to* TANIA *that she should leave the room. She does so, irritably.* SALIM *tries to take her hand as she goes but she pulls away from him. She has gone now.*)

(*To* OMAR) You like Tania?

OMAR: Oh yes.

NASSER: I'll see what I can do.

(ZAKI *laughs and slaps* OMAR *on the knee.* OMAR *is uncomprehending.*)

To business now. I went to see the laundrette. You boys will make a beautiful job of it, I know. You need nothing more from there. (*To* OMAR.) But in exchange I want you

to do something. You look like a tough chap. I've got some
bastard tenants in one of my houses I can't get rid of.

JOHNNY: No, I don't do nothing rough no more.

NASSER: I'm not looking for a mass murderer, you bloody fool.

JOHNNY: What's it involve, please?

NASSER: I tell you. Unscrewing. (*To* SALIM.) We're on your
favourite subject.

SALIM: For Christ's sake!

JOHNNY: What is unscrewing?

ZAKI: You're getting into some family business, that's all.

SALIM: What the hell else is there for them in this country now?

NASSER: (*To* OMAR) Send him to my garage. And call Tania to
bring us champagne. And we'll drink to Thatcher and your
beautiful laundrette.

JOHNNY: Do they go together?

NASSER: Like dall and chipatis!

EXT. OUTSIDE THE LAUNDRETTE. NIGHT

JOHNNY *and* OMAR *have parked their car by the laundrette. They
lean against the car, close together, talking.*

JOHNNY: The timber's coming tomorrow morning. I'm getting
it cheap.

(*They walk slowly towards the laundrette.*)

OMAR: I've had a vision. Of how this place could be. Why do
people hate laundrettes? Because they're like toilets. This
could be a Ritz among laundrettes.

JOHNNY: A laundrette as big as the Ritz. Yeah.

(JOHNNY *puts his arm round* OMAR. OMAR *turns to him and
they kiss on the mouth. They kiss passionately and hold each
other.*

On the other side of the laundrette, GENGHIS, MOOSE *and
three other* LADS *are kicking the laundrette dustbins across the
pavement. They can't see* OMAR *and* JOHNNY.

JOHNNY *detaches himself from* OMAR *and walks round the
laundrette to the* LADS. OMAR *moves into a position from where
he can see, but doesn't approach the* LADS.

MOOSE *sees* JOHNNY *and motions to* GENGHIS *who is
engrossed with the kicking.* GENGHIS *faces* JOHNNY. JOHNNY
controls himself. He straightens the dustbin and starts banging

the rubbish back in. He gestures to a couple of the LADS *to help him. They move back, away from him.*

JOHNNY *grabs* MOOSE *by the hair and stuffs his head into a dustbin.* MOOSE, *suitably disciplined, then helps* JOHNNY *stuff the rubbish back in the bin, looking guiltily at* GENGHIS.)

GENGHIS: Why are you working for them? For these people? You were with us once. For England.

JOHNNY: It's work. I want to work. I'm fed up of hanging about.

GENGHIS: I'm angry. I don't like to see one of our men grovelling to Pakis. They came here to work for us. That's why we brought them over. OK?

(*And* GENGHIS *moves away. As he does so, he sees* OMAR. *The others see him at the same time.* MOOSE *takes out a knife.* GENGHIS *indicates for him to keep back. He wants to concentrate on* JOHNNY.)

Don't cut yourself off from your own people. Because there's no one else who really wants you. Everyone has to belong.

EXT. SOUTH LONDON STREET. NIGHT

They are in a street of desolate semi-detached houses in bad condition, ready for demolition. JOHNNY *kisses* OMAR *and opens the car door.*

JOHNNY: I can't ask you in. And you'd better get back to your father.

OMAR: I didn't think you'd ever mention my father.

JOHNNY: He helped me, didn't he? When I was at school.

OMAR: And what did you do but hurt him?

JOHNNY: I want to forget all of those things.

(*He gets out quickly and walks across the front of the car. He turns the corner of the street.* OMAR *gets out of the car and follows him.*)

EXT. STREET. NIGHT

OMAR *follows* JOHNNY, *making sure he isn't seen.*

JOHNNY *turns into a boarded-up derelict house.* OMAR *watches him go round the side of the house and climb in through a broken door.*

OMAR *turns away.*

INT. PAPA'S FLAT. NIGHT

PAPA *is asleep in the room, dead drunk and snoring.* OMAR *has come in. He stands by Papa's bed and strokes his head.*

He picks up an almost empty bottle of vodka and drinks from it, finishing it. He goes to the balcony door with it.

EXT. BALCONY. NIGHT

OMAR *stands on the balcony, looking over the silent railway line. Then, suddenly, he shouts joyfully into the distance. And throws the empty bottle as far as he can.*

EXT. OUTSIDE THE LAUNDRETTE. DAY

OMAR *and* JOHNNY *are working hard and with great concentration, painting the outside of the laundrette, the doors, etc. Although it's not finished, it's beginning to reach its final state. The new windows have been installed; but the neon sign isn't yet up.*

KIDS *play football nearby. And various cynical* LOCALS *watch, a couple of* OLD MEN *whom we see in the betting shop later. Also* MOOSE *and another* LAD *who are amused by all the effort. They lean against a wall opposite and drink from cans.*

Further up the street SALIM *is watching all this from his parked car.*

JOHNNY *is up a ladder. He gets down the ladder, nods goodbye to* OMAR *and puts his paint brush away.* SALIM *reverses his car.*

JOHNNY *walks away.* OMAR *looks nervously across at* MOOSE *who stares at him.*

INT. GARAGE OFFICE. DAY

NASSER *and* SALIM *in the glassed-in office of the garage.* NASSER *is going through various papers on his desk.* SALIM *watches him and is very persistent.*

SALIM: I passed by the laundrette. So you gave them money to do it up? (NASSER *shakes his head.*) Where did they get it from, I wonder?

NASSER: Government grant. (SALIM *looks dubiously at* NASSER.) Oh, Omo's like us, yaar. Doesn't he fit with us like a glove? He's pure bloody family. (*Looks knowingly at* SALIM.) So, like you, God knows what he's doing for money. (NASSER *looks up and sees* JOHNNY *squashing his face against the glass of the door of the office. He starts to laugh.*)

SALIM: That other joker's a bad influence on Omo. I'm sure of it. There's some things between them I'm looking into.
(JOHNNY *comes in.*)
(*To* OMAR) So they let you out of prison. Too crowded, are they?
JOHNNY: Unscrew.
(SALIM *reacts.* NASSER *quickly leads* JOHNNY *out of the office, while speaking to* SALIM *through the open door.*)
NASSER: (*In Urdu*) Don't worry, I'm just putting this bastard to work.
SALIM: (*In Urdu*) The bastard, it's a job in itself.
NASSER: (*In Urdu*) I'll have my foot up his arse at all times.
SALIM: (*In Urdu*) That's exactly how they like it. And he'll steal your boot too.
(JOHNNY *looks amusedly at them both.*)

INT. HOUSE. DAY
This is one of Nasser's properties. A falling-down four-storey place in South London, the rooms of which he rents out to itinerants and students.
Peeling walls, faded carpets, cat piss. JOHNNY *and* NASSER *are on the top landing of the house, standing by a door.* JOHNNY *is holding a tool kit, which he starts to unpack.*
NASSER: He's changed the lock so you take off the whole door in case he changes it again. He's only a poet with no money.
JOHNNY: I'm not hurting nobody, OK?

INT. TOP CORRIDOR OF HOUSE. DAY
Later. NASSER *has gone.* JOHNNY *has got through the lock and the door is open. He is unscrewing the hinges and singing to himself.*
At the end of the hall a Pakistani in his fifties watches him.
JOHNNY *lifts the door off the frame and leans it against the wall.*
POET: Now that door you've just taken off. Hang it back.
(*With great grunting effort* JOHNNY *picks the door up. He tries hard to move past the* POET *with it. The* POET *shoves* JOHNNY *hard.* JOHNNY *almost balances himself again but not quite, does a kind of dance with the door before crashing over with it on top of him.*)

40

JOHNNY *struggles to his feet. The* POET *advances towards him and* JOHNNY *retreats.*)
I'm a poor man. This is my room. Let's leave it that way.
(*And the* POET *shoves* JOHNNY *again.*

JOHNNY, *not wanting to resist, falls against the wall.*

At the end of the hall, at the top of the stairs, NASSER *appears. The* POET *turns to* NASSER *and moves towards him, abusing him in Punjabi.* NASSER *ignores him. As the* POET *goes for* NASSER, JOHNNY *grabs the* POET *from behind and twists his arm up behind him.*)

NASSER: Throw this bugger out!

(JOHNNY *shoves the struggling* POET *along the corridor to the top of the stairs and then bundles him downstairs.*)

INT. ROOM. DAY
The room from which JOHNNY *removed the door. A large badly furnished bedsit with a cooker, fridge, double-bed, wardrobe, etc.*

NASSER *is giving* JOHNNY *money. Then* NASSER *opens the window and looks out down the street. The* POET *is walking away from the house.* NASSER *calls out after him in Punjabi. And he throws the poet's things out of the window. The* POET *scrabbles around down below, gathering his things.*)

JOHNNY: Aren't you giving ammunition to your enemies doing this kind of . . . unscrewing? To people who say Pakis just come here to hustle other people's lives and jobs and houses.

NASSER: But we're professional businessmen. Not professional Pakistanis. There's no race question in the new enterprise culture. Do you like the room? Omar said you had nowhere to live. I won't charge.

JOHNNY: Why not?

NASSER: You can unscrew. That's confirmed beautifully. But can you unblock and can you keep this zoo here under control? Eh?

EXT. LAUNDRETTE. EVENING
Music.

JOHNNY *is working on the outside of the laundrette. He's fixing up the neon sign, on his own, and having difficulty.* OMAR *stands*

41

*down below, expensively dressed, not willing to assist. Across the
street* MOOSE *and a couple of* LADS *are watching.*

OMAR: I wish Salim could see this.

JOHNNY: Why? He's on to us. Oh yeah, he's just biding his
time. Then he'll get us.

> (*He indicates to* MOOSE. MOOSE *comes over and helps him.*
>
> The OLD MEN *are watching wisely as* JOHNNY *and* MOOSE
> *precariously sway on a board suspended across two ladders,
> while holding the neon sign saying POWDERS.*)

OMAR: You taking the room in Nasser's place?

> (*A ball is kicked by the* KIDS *which whistles past* JOHNNY *'s
> ear.* MOOSE *reacts.*)

Make sure you pay the rent. Otherwise you'll have to
chuck yourself out of the window.

> (GENGHIS *walks down the street towards the laundrette.* OMAR
> *turns and goes.*
>
> MOOSE *goes into a panic, knowing* GENGHIS *will be furious
> at this act of collaboration.* JOHNNY *glances at* MOOSE.
>
> GENGHIS *is coming. The ladders sway. And the* OLD MEN
> *watch.* GENGHIS *stops.* MOOSE *looks at him.*)

INT. LAUNDRETTE. DAY

The day of the opening of the laundrette.

> *The laundrette is finished. And the place looks terrific: pot plants;
> a TV on which videos are showing; a sound system; and the place is
> brightly painted and clean.*
>
> OMAR *is splendidly dressed. He is walking round the place, drink
> in hand, looking it over.*
>
> *Outside, local people look in curiously and press their faces against
> the glass. Two old ladies are patiently waiting to be let in. A queue of
> people with washing gradually forms.*
>
> *In the open door of the back room* JOHNNY *is changing into his
> new clothes.*

OMAR: Let's open. The world's waiting.

OMAR: I've invited Nasser to the launch. And Papa's coming.
They're not here yet. Papa hasn't been out for months. We
can't move till he arrives.

JOHNNY: What time did they say they'd be here?

OMAR: An hour ago.

JOHNNY: They're not gonna come, then.
>(OMAR *looks hurt.* JOHNNY *indicates that* OMAR *should go to him. He goes to him.*)

INT. BACK ROOM OF LAUNDRETTE. DAY
The back room has also been done up, in a bright high-tech style. And a two-way mirror has been installed, through which they can see into the laundrette.
>OMAR *watches* JOHNNY, *sitting on the desk.*

JOHNNY: Shall I open the champagne then? (*He opens the bottle.*)

OMAR: Didn't I predict this? (*They look through the mirror and through the huge windows of the laundrette to the patient punters waiting outside.*) This whole stinking area's on its knees begging for clean clothes. Jesus Christ.
>(OMAR *touches his own shoulders.* JOHNNY *massages him.*)

JOHNNY: Let's open up.

OMAR: Not till Papa comes. Remember? He went out of his way with you. And with all my friends. (*Suddenly harsh.*) He did, didn't he!

JOHNNY: Omo. What are you on about, mate?

OMAR: About how years later he saw the same boys. And what were they doing?

JOHNNY: What?

OMAR: What were they doing on marches through Lewisham? It was bricks and bottles and Union Jacks. It was immigrants out. It was kill us. People we knew. And it was you. He saw you marching. You saw his face, watching you. Don't deny it. We were there when you went past. (OMAR *is being held by* JOHNNY, *in his arms.*) Papa hated himself and his job. He was afraid on the street for me. And he took it out on her. And she couldn't bear it. Oh, such failure, such emptiness.
>(JOHNNY *kisses* OMAR *then leaves him, sitting away from him slightly.* OMAR *touches him, asking him to hold him.*)

INT. LAUNDRETTE. DAY
NASSER *and* RACHEL *stride enthusiastically into the not yet open laundrette, carrying paper cups and a bottle of whisky. Modern music suitable for waltzing to is playing.*

NASSER: What a beautiful thing they've done with it! Isn't it?
      Oh, God and with music too!
RACHEL: It's like an incredible ship. I had no idea.
NASSER: He's a marvellous bloody boy, Rachel, I tell you.
RACHEL: You don't have to tell me.
NASSER: But I tell you everything five times.
RACHEL: At least.
NASSER: Am I a bad man to you then?
RACHEL: You are sometimes . . . careless.
NASSER: (*Moved*) Yes.
RACHEL: Dance with me. (*He goes to her.*) But we are learning.
NASSER: Where are those two buggers?

INT. BACK ROOM OF LAUNDRETTE. DAY
OMAR *and* JOHNNY *are holding each other.*
JOHNNY: Nothing I can say, to make it up to you. There's only
      things I can do to show that I am . . . with you.
      (OMAR *starts to unbutton* JOHNNY'*s shirt.*)

INT. LAUNDRETTE. DAY
NASSER *and* RACHEL *are waltzing across the laundrette. Outside,
the old ladies are shifting about impatiently.*
NASSER: Of course, Johnny did all the physical work on this.
RACHEL: You're fond of him.
NASSER: I wish I could do something more to help the other
      deadbeat children like him. They hang about the road like
      pigeons, making a mess, doing nothing.
RACHEL: And you're tired of work.
NASSER: It's time I became a holy man.
RACHEL: A sadhu of South London.
NASSER: (*Surprised at her knowledge*) Yes. But first I must marry
      Omar off.

INT. BACK ROOM OF LAUNDRETTE. DAY
OMAR *and* JOHNNY *are making love vigorously, enjoying themselves
thoroughly. Suddenly* OMAR *stops a moment, looks up, sees* NASSER
and RACHEL *waltzing across the laundrette.* OMAR *jumps up.*

44

INT. LAUNDRETTE. DAY
NASSER *strides impatiently towards the door of the back room.*

INT. BACK ROOM OF LAUNDRETTE. DAY
OMAR *and* JOHNNY *are quickly getting dressed.* NASSER *bursts into the room.*
NASSER: What the hell are you doing? Sunbathing?
OMAR: Asleep, Uncle. We were shagged out. Where's Papa?
 (NASSER *just looks at* OMAR. RACHEL *appears at the door behind him.*)

INT. LAUNDRETTE. DAY
The laundrette is open now. The ladies and other locals are doing their washing. The machines are whirring, sheets are being folded, magazines read, music played, video games played, etc.
 SALIM *arrives with* ZAKI. *They talk as they come in.*
ZAKI: Laundrettes are impossible. I've got two laundrettes and two ulcers. Plus . . . piles!
 (GENGHIS, MOOSE *and the rest of the gang arrive.* MOOSE *goes into the laundrette, followed by* GENGHIS. GENGHIS *turns and forbids the rest of the* GANG *from entering. They wait restlessly outside.*
 JOHNNY *is talking to* RACHEL.)
RACHEL: What's your surname?
JOHNNY: Burfoot.
RACHEL: That's it. I know your mother.
 (*The* TELEPHONE CHARACTER *is on the phone, talking eagerly to his Angela.*
 Through the window, OMAR, *who is talking to* NASSER, *sees* TANIA. *She is crossing the road and carrying a bouquet of flowers.*)
OMAR: I thought Papa just might make it today, Uncle.
NASSER: He said he never visits laundrettes.
 (TANIA *comes in through the door.*)
JOHNNY: (*To* RACHEL) Oh good, it's Tania.
RACHEL: I've never met her. But she has a beautiful face.
 (JOHNNY *leaves* RACHEL *and goes to* TANIA, *kissing her. He takes the flowers delightedly.*
 NASSER *is disturbed by the sudden unexpected appearance of*

his daughter, since he is with his mistress, RACHEL.)

NASSER: (*To* OMAR) Who invited Tania, dammit?

(GENGHIS *and* MOOSE *shout out as they play the video game.*)

OMAR: I did, Uncle.

(*They watch as* TANIA *goes to* RACHEL *with* JOHNNY.

JOHNNY *has no choice but to introduce* TANIA *and* RACHEL.)

TANIA: (*Smiles at* RACHEL) At last. After so many years in my family's life.

RACHEL: Tania, I do feel I know you.

TANIA: But you don't.

NASSER: (*Watching this*) Bring Tania over here.

TANIA: (*To* RACHEL) I don't mind my father having a mistress.

RACHEL: Good. I am so grateful.

NASSER: (*To* OMAR) Then marry her. (OMAR *looks at him.*) What's wrong with her? If I say marry her then you damn well do it!

TANIA: (*To* RACHEL) I don't mind my father spending our money on you.

RACHEL: Why don't you mind?

NASSER: (*To* OMAR) Start being nice to Tania. Take the pressure off my fucking head.

TANIA: (*To* RACHEL) Or my father being with you instead of with our mother.

NASSER: (*To* OMAR) Your penis works, doesn't it?

TANIA: (*To* RACHEL) But I don't like women who live off men.

NASSER: (*Shoving* OMAR *forward*) Get going then!

TANIA: (*To* RACHEL) That's a pretty disgusting parasitical thing, isn't it?

OMAR: (*To* TANIA) Tania, come and look at the spin-driers. They are rather interesting.

RACHEL: But tell me, who do you live off? And you must understand, we are of different generations, and different classes. Everything is waiting for you. The only thing that has ever waited for me is your father.

(*Then, with great dignity,* NASSER *goes to* RACHEL.)

NASSER: We'd better get going. See you boys.

(*He shakes hands warmly with* OMAR *and* JOHNNY. *And goes out with* RACHEL, *ignoring* TANIA.

Outside in the street, RACHEL *and* NASSER *begin to argue*

bitterly. They are watched by the rest of the GANG. RACHEL
and NASSER *finally walk away from each other, in different
directions, sadly.*)

INT. LAUNDRETTE. DAY
*The laundrette is full now, mostly with real punters doing their
washing and enjoying being there.*

GENGHIS *and* MOOSE *are still drinking.* GENGHIS *talks across the
laundrette to* JOHNNY. JOHNNY *is doing a service wash, folding
clothes.*

OMAR *is saying goodbye to* TANIA *at the door.*

SALIM *has hung back and is waiting for* OMAR, ZAKI *says goodbye
to him and goes, tentatively past the volatile breast-baring* TANIA.

TANIA: (*To* OMAR) I want to leave home. I need to break away.
      You'll have to help me financially.
      (OMAR *nods enthusiastically.*)

GENGHIS: (*To* JOHNNY) Why don't you come out with us no
      more?

OMAR: (*To* TANIA) I'm drunk.

JOHNNY: (*To* GENGHIS) I'm busy here full-time, Genghis.

OMAR: (*To* TANIA) Will you marry me, Tania?

TANIA: (*To* OMAR) If you can get me some money.

GENGHIS: (*To* JOHNNY) Don't the Paki give you time off?

MOOSE: (*To* JOHNNY) I bet you ain't got the guts to ask him for
      time off.

SALIM: (*To* JOHNNY, *indicating* OMAR) Omo's getting married.
      (TANIA *goes.* SALIM *goes to* OMAR. *He puts his arm round him
      and takes him outside.* OMAR *is reluctant to go at first, but*
      SALIM *is firm and strong and pulls him out.* JOHNNY *watches.*)

GENGHIS: (*To* JOHNNY) You out with us tonight then?

EXT. STREET OUTSIDE LAUNDRETTE. DAY
It is starting to get dark. OMAR *and* SALIM *stand beside Salim's
smart car.*

Eager and curious customers are still arriving. SALIM *nods
approvingly at them.*

*Above them the huge pink flashing neon sign saying
'POWDERS'.*

Some kids are playing football in the street opposite the laundrette.

JOHNNY *rushes to the door of the laundrette. He shouts at the kids.*

JOHNNY: You mind these windows!

> (SALIM, *being watched by* JOHNNY, *starts to lead* OMAR *up the street, away from the laundrette.*)

SALIM: (*To* OMAR) I'm afraid you owe me a lot of money. The beard? Remember? Eh? Good. It's all coming back. I think I'd better have that money back, don't you?

OMAR: I haven't got money like that now.

SALIM: Because it's all in the laundrette?

> (GENGHIS *and* MOOSE *have come out of the laundrette and walked up the street away from it, parallel with* OMAR *and* SALIM. GENGHIS *stares contemptuously at* SALIM *and* MOOSE *spits on the pavement.* SALIM *ignores them.*)

I'd better have a decent down payment then, of about half. (OMAR *nods.*) By the time Nasser has his annual party, say. Or I'll instruct him to get rid of the laundrette. You see, if anyone does anything wrong with me, I always destroy them.

> (JOHNNY *comes out of the laundrette and runs up behind* GENGHIS *and* MOOSE, *jumping on* MOOSE'*s back. They turn the corner, away from* SALIM *and* OMAR. OMAR *watches them go anxiously, not understanding what* JOHNNY *could be doing with them.*)

OMAR: Took you a while to get on to us.

SALIM: Wanted to see what you'd do. How's your Papa? (OMAR *shrugs.*) So many books written and read. Politicians sought him out. Bhutto was his close friend. But we're nothing in England without money.

INT. BETTING SHOP. DAY

There are only five or six people in the betting shop, all of them men.

And the men are mostly old, in slippers and filthy suits; with bandaged legs and stained shirts and unshaven milk-bottle-white faces and National Health glasses. NASSER *looks confident and powerful beside them. He knows them. There's a good sense of camaraderie amongst them.*

When OMAR *goes into the betting shop* NASSER *is sitting on a stool, a pile of betting slips in front of him, staring at one of the newspaper pages pinned to the wall. An* OLD MAN *is sitting next to* NASSER, *giving him advice.*

OMAR *goes to* NASSER.

OMAR: (*Anxiously*) Uncle. (NASSER *ignores him.*) Uncle.

NASSER: (*Scribbling on betting slip*) Even royalty can't reach me in the afternoons.

OMAR: I've got to talk. About Salim.

NASSER: Is he squeezing your balls?

OMAR: Yes. I want your help, Uncle.

NASSER: (*Getting up*) You do it all now. It's up to you, boy.

(NASSER *goes to the betting counter and hands over his betting slips. He also hands over a thick pile of money.*

Over the shop PA we can hear that the race is beginning. It starts.

NASSER *listens as if hypnotized, staring wildly at the others in the shop, for sympathy, clenching his fists, stamping his feet and shouting loudly as his horse, 'Elvis', is among the front runners.*

OMAR *has never seen* NASSER *like this before.*)

(*To horse*) Come on, Elvis, my son. (*To* OMAR.) You'll just have to run the whole family yourself now. (*To horse.*) Go on, boy! (*To* OMAR.) You take control. (*To horse and others in shop.*) Yes, yes, yes, he's going to take it, the little bastard black beauty! (*To* OMAR.) It's all yours. Salim too. (*To horse.*) Do it, do it, do it, baby! No, no, no, no.

(NASSER *is rigid with self-loathing and disappointment as 'Elvis' loses the race. The betting slip falls from his hand. And he hangs his head in despair.*)

OMAR: Where's Rachel?

NASSER: You can't talk to her. She's busy pulling her hair out. If only your damn father were sober. I'd talk to him about her. He's the only one who knows anything. (*Facetious.*) I'd ask him about Salim if I were you.

(OMAR *stares at* NASSER *in fury and disgust. He storms out of the betting shop, just as the next race . . . a dog race . . . is about to start.*)

INT. LAUNDRETTE. EVENING

The laundrette is fully functional now, busy and packed with customers.

Music is playing – a soprano aria from **Madam Butterfly**.

Customers are reading magazines. They are talking, watching TV with the sound turned down and one white man is singing along with the Puccini which he knows word for word.

The TELEPHONE CHARACTER *is yelling into the bright new yellow phone.*

TELEPHONE CHARACTER: (*Into phone*) 'Course I'll look after it! I'll come round every other night. At least. Honest. I want children!

(OMAR *walks around the laundrette, watching over it, proud and stern. He helps people if the doors of the renovated machines are stiff.*

And he hands people baskets to move their washing about in. Shots of people putting money into the machines.

But JOHNNY *isn't there.* OMAR *doesn't know where he is and looks outside anxiously for him. He is worried and upset about Salim's demand for money.*

Finally, OMAR *goes out into the street and asks a kid if he's seen* JOHNNY.)

INT. TOP HALL OF THE HOUSE JOHNNY'S MOVED INTO. NIGHT
A party is going on in one of the rooms on this floor. The noise is tremendous and people are falling about the hall.

A PAKISTANI STUDENT, *a man in his late twenties with an intelligent face, is bent over someone who has collapsed across the doorway between room and hall.*

PAKISTANI STUDENT: (*As* OMAR *goes past*) There's only one word for your uncle. (OMAR *walks on fastidiously, ignoring them, to Johnny's door. The* STUDENT *yells.*) Collaborator with the white man!

(OMAR *knocks on Johnny's door.*)

INT. JOHNNY'S ROOM. NIGHT
OMAR *goes into Johnny's room.* JOHNNY *is lying on the bed, drinking, wearing a pair of boxer shorts.*

OMAR *stands at the open door.*

JOHNNY *runs to the door and screams up the hall to the*
PAKISTANI STUDENT.

JOHNNY: Didn't I tell you, didn't I tell you 'bout that noise last night? (*Pause.*) Well, didn't I?

(*The* PAKISTANI STUDENT *stares contemptuously at him. The drunks lie where they are.* JOHNNY *slams the door of his room. And* OMAR *starts on him.*)

OMAR: Where did you go? You just disappeared!

JOHNNY: Drinking, I went. With me old mates. It's not illegal.

OMAR: 'Course it is. Laundrettes are a big commitment. Why aren't you at work?

JOHNNY: It'll be closing time soon. You'll be locking the place up, and coming to bed.

OMAR: No, it never closes. And one of us has got to be there. That way we begin to make money.

JOHNNY: You're getting greedy.

OMAR: I want big money. I'm not gonna be beat down by this country. When we were at school, you and your lot kicked me all round the place. And what are you doing now? Washing my floor. That's how I like it. Now get to work. Get to work I said. Or you're fired!

(OMAR *grabs him and pulls him up.* JOHNNY *doesn't resist.* OMAR *throws his shirt and shoes at him.* JOHNNY *dresses.*)

JOHNNY: (*Touching him*) What about you?

OMAR: I don't wanna see you for a little while. I got some big thinking to do.

(JOHNNY *looks regretfully at him.*)

JOHNNY: But today, it's been the best day!

OMAR: Yeah. Almost the best day.

INT. TOP HALL. NIGHT

JOHNNY, *dressed now, walks past the party room. The* PAKISTANI STUDENT *is now playing a tabla in the hall.* JOHNNY *ignores him, though the student looks ironically at him.*

INT. BOTTOM ENTRANCE HALL OF THE HOUSE, NIGHT

JOHNNY *stops by a wall box in the hall. He pulls a bunch of keys out of his pocket and unlocks the wall box.*

He reaches in and pulls a switch.

INT. OUTSIDE THE HOUSE. NIGHT

JOHNNY *walks away from the house. He has plunged the party room into darkness. In the room people are screaming.*

The PAKISTANI STUDENT *yells out of the window at* JOHNNY.

PAKISTANI STUDENT: You are not human! You are cold people, you English, the big icebergs of Europe!

(OMAR *stands at the next window along, looking out. This room is lighted.*

JOHNNY *chuckles to himself as he walks jauntily away.*)

INT. LAUNDRETTE. NIGHT

Nina Simone's smooth 'Walk On By' playing in the laundrette.

And there are still plenty of people around.

The TELEPHONE CHARACTER *has turned to the wall, head down, to concentrate on his conversation.*

A MAN *is asleep on a bench.* JOHNNY *walks past him, notices he's asleep and suddenly pokes him. The* MAN *jumps awake.* JOHNNY *points at the man's washing.*

A young black COUPLE *are dancing, holding each other sleepily as they wait for their washing.*

A BUM *comes in through the door, slowly, with difficulty in walking. He's wearing a large black overcoat with the collar turned up.* JOHNNY *watches him.*

JOHNNY: Hey!

(*The* BUM *doesn't respond.* JOHNNY *goes to him and takes his arm, about to chuck him out. Then the* BUM *turns to* JOHNNY.)

PAPA: I recognize you at least. Let me sit.

(JOHNNY *leads* PAPA *up the laundrette.*

The TELEPHONE CHARACTER *throws down the receiver and walks out.*)

JOHNNY: (*Deferential now*) We were expecting you today.

PAPA: I've come.

JOHNNY: The invitation was for two o'clock, Mr Ali.

PAPA: (*Looking at his watch*) It's only ten past now. I thought I'd come to the wrong place. That I was suddenly in the ladies' hairdressing salon in Pinner, where one might get a pink rinse. Do you do a pink rinse, Johnny? Or are you still a fascist?

JOHNNY: You used to give me a lot of good advice, sir. When I was little.

PAPA: When you were little. What's it made of you? Are you a politician? Journalist? A trade unionist? No, you are an underpants cleaner. (*Self-mocking.*) Oh dear, the working class are such a great disappointment to me.

JOHNNY: I haven't made much of myself.

PAPA: You'd better get on and do something.

JOHNNY: Yes. Here, we can do something.

PAPA: Help me. I want my son out of this underpants cleaning condition. I want him reading in college. You tell him: you go to college. He must have knowledge. We all must, now. In order to see clearly what's being done and to whom in this country. Right?

JOHNNY: I don't know. It depends on what he wants.

PAPA: No. (*Strongly.*) You must use your influence. (PAPA *gets up and walks out slowly.* JOHNNY *watches him go, sadly.* PAPA *turns.*) Not a bad dump you got here.

EXT. OUTSIDE THE LAUNDRETTE. NIGHT
PAPA *walks away from the laundrette.*

EXT. THE DRIVE OF NASSER'S HOUSE. DAY
JOHNNY *has come by bus to Nasser's house. And* OMAR *opens the front door to him.* JOHNNY *is about to step into the house.* OMAR *takes him out into the drive.*

JOHNNY: What you make me come all this way for?

OMAR: Gotta talk.

JOHNNY: You bloody arse. (*At the side of the house a strange sight.* TANIA *is climbing a tree.* BILQUIS *is at the bottom of the tree yelling instructions to her in Urdu.* JOHNNY *and* OMAR *watch.*) What's going on?

OMAR: It's heavy, man. Bilquis is making magical potions from leaves and bird beaks and stuff. She's putting them on Rachel.

(JOHNNY *watches* TANIA *groping for leaves in amazement.*)

JOHNNY: Is it working?

OMAR: Rachel rang me. She's got the vicar round. He's performing an exorcism right now. The furniture's shaking. Her trousers are walking by themselves.

INT. NASSER'S ROOM. DAY
OMAR *and* JOHNNY *and* NASSER *are sitting at a table in Nasser's room, playing cards.* TANIA *is sulky. He puts his cards down.*
NASSER: I'm out.
> (*He gets up and goes and lies down on the bed, his arm over his face.*
>> OMAR *and* JOHNNY *continue playing. They put their cards down.* JOHNNY *wins. He collects the money.*)

OMAR: Salim's gotta have money. Soon. A lot of money. He threatened me. (*They get up and walk out of the room, talking in low voices.* NASSER *lies there on the bed, not listening but brooding.*) I didn't wanna tell you before. I thought I could raise the money on the profits from the laundrette. But it's impossible in the time.

INT. HALL OUTSIDE NASSER'S ROOM. DAY
They walk down the hall to the verandah.
JOHNNY: This city's chock-full of money. When I used to want money –
OMAR: You'd steal it.
JOHNNY: Yeah. Decide now if you want it to be like that again.

INT. VERANDAH. DAY
They reach the verandah. Outside, in the garden, the two younger DAUGHTERS *are playing.*
> *At the other end of the verandah* BILQUIS *and* TANIA *are sitting on the sofa, a table in front of them.* BILQUIS *is mixing various ingredients in a big bowl – vegetables, bits of bird, leaves, some dog urine, the squeezed eyeball of a newt, half a goldfish, etc. We see her slicing the goldfish.*
> *At the same time she is dictating a letter to* TANIA, *which* TANIA *takes down on a blue airletter.* TANIA *looks pretty fed-up.*
>> OMAR *and* JOHNNY *sit down and watch them.*
JOHNNY: She's illiterate. Tania's writing to her sister for her. Bilquis is thinking of going back, after she's hospitalized Rachel. (BILQUIS *looks up at them, her eyes dark and her face humourless.*) Nasser's embarked on a marathon sulk. He's going for the world record.
> (*Pause.* JOHNNY *changes the subject back when* TANIA –

suspecting them of laughing at her – gives them a sharp look.)
JOHNNY: We'll just have to do a job to get the money.
OMAR: I don't want you going back to all that.
JOHNNY: Just to get us through, Omo. It's for both of us. If
we're going to go on. You want that, don't you?
OMAR: Yes. I want you.
(*Suddenly* NASSER *appears at the door and starts abusing*
BILQUIS *in loud Urdu, telling her that the magic business is*
stupid, etc. But BILQUIS *has a rougher, louder tongue. She*
says, among other things, in Urdu, that NASSER *is a big fat*
black man who should get out of her sight for ever.

TANIA *is very distressed by this, hands over face. Suddenly*
she gets up. The magic potion bowl is knocked over, the evil
ingredients spilling over Bilquis' feet. BILQUIS *screams.*
JOHNNY *starts laughing.* BILQUIS *picks up the rest of the bowl*
and throws the remainder of the potion over NASSER.)

INT. OUTSIDE A SMART HOUSE. NIGHT
A semi-detached house. A hedge around the front of the house.
JOHNNY *is forcing the front window. He knows what he's doing.*
He climbs in. He indicates to OMAR *that he should follow. And*
OMAR *follows.*

INT. FRONT ROOM OF THE HOUSE. NIGHT
They're removing the video and TV and going out the front door
with them. Their car is parked outside.
Suddenly a tiny KID *of about eight is standing behind them at the*
bottom of the stairs. He is an INDIAN KID. OMAR *looks at him, the*
KID *opens his mouth to yell.* OMAR *grabs the* KID *and slams his*
hand over his mouth. While he holds the KID, JOHNNY *goes out*
with the stereo. Then the compact disc player.
OMAR *leaves the stunned* KID *and makes a run for it.*

INT. BACK ROOM OF LAUNDRETTE. NIGHT
There are televisions, stereos, radios, videos, etc. stacked up in the
back room. OMAR *stands there looking at them.*
JOHNNY *comes in struggling with a video.* OMAR *smiles at him.*
JOHNNY *doesn't respond.*

INT. HALL. DAY

The top hall of the house JOHNNY *lives in.* JOHNNY, *wearing jeans and T-shirt, barefoot, only recently having woken up, is banging on the door of the Pakistani student's room.*

OMAR *is standing beside him, smartly dressed and carrying a briefcase. He's spent the night with* JOHNNY. *And now he's going to the laundrette.*

JOHNNY: (*To door*) Rent day! Rent up, man!

> (OMAR *watches him.* JOHNNY *looks unhappy.*)

OMAR: I said it would bring you down, stealing again. It's no good for you. You need a brand new life.

> (*The* PAKISTANI STUDENT *opens the door.* OMAR *moves away. To* JOHNNY.) Party tonight. then we'll be in the clear.

PAKISTANI STUDENT: Unblock the toilet, yes, Johnny?

JOHNNY: (*Looking into the room*) Tonight. You're not doing nothing political in there, are you, man? I've gotta take a look.

> (OMAR, *laughing, moves away.* JOHNNY *shoves the door hard and the* PAKISTANI STUDENT *relents.*)

INT. PAKISTANI STUDENT'S ROOM. DAY

JOHNNY *goes into the room. A young* PAKISTANI STUDENT *is sitting on the bed with a* CHILD.

A younger PAKISTANI BOY *of about fourteen is standing behind her. And across the room a* PAKISTANI GIRL *of seventeen.*

PAKISTANI STUDENT: My family, escaping persecution.

> (JOHNNY *looks at him.*) Are you a good man or are you a bad man?

EXT. COUNTRY LANE AND DRIVE OF NASSER'S HOUSE. EVENING

OMAR *and* JOHNNY *are sitting in the back of a mini-cab.*

JOHNNY *is as dressed up as is* OMAR, *but in fashionable street clothes rather than an expensive dark suit.* JOHNNY *will be out of keeping sartorially with the rest of the party.*

The young ASIAN DRIVER *moves the car towards Nasser's house.*

The house is a blaze of light and noise. And the drive is full of cars and PAKISTANIS *and* INDIANS *getting noisily out of them. Looking at the house, the lights, the extravagance,* JOHNNY *laughs sarcastically.*

> OMAR, *paying the driver, looks irritably at* JOHNNY.

JOHNNY: What does he reckon he is, your uncle? Some kinda big Gatsby geezer((OMAR *gives him a cutting look.*) Maybe this just isn't my world. You're right. Still getting married? (*They both get out of the car.* OMAR *walks towards the house.* JOHNNY *stands there a moment, not wanting to face it all.*

> When OMAR *has almost reached the front door and* TANIA *has come out to hug him,* JOHNNY *moves towards the house.*

> TANIA *hugs* JOHNNY.

> OMAR *looks into the house and sees* SALIM *and* CHERRY *in the crowd in the front room. He waves at* SALIM *but* SALIM *ignores him.* CHERRY *is starting to look pregnant.*

> BILQUIS *is standing at the end of the hall. She greets* OMAR *in Urdu. And he replies in rudimentary Urdu.*

> JOHNNY *feels rather odd since he's the only white person in sight.*)

INT./EXT. THE VERANDAH, PATIO AND GARDEN. EVENING
The house, patio and garden are full of well-off, well-dressed, well-pissed, middle-class PAKISTANIS *and* INDIANS.

The American, DICK, *and the* ENGLISHMAN *are talking together.*

DICK: England needs more young men like Omar and Johnny, from what I can see.

ENGLISHMAN: (*Slightly camp*) The more boys like that the better.

> (*We see* OMAR *on the verandah talking confidently to various people. Occasionally he glances at* SALIM *who is engrossed in conversation with* ZAKI *and Zaki's* WIFE. *A snatch of their conversation.*

NASSER: Now Cherry is pregnant I will be buying a house. I am going to have many children . . .

> (BILQUIS *is there. She is alone but there is a fierceness and cheerfulness about her that we haven't noticed before.*

> JOHNNY *doesn't know who to talk to.* CHERRY *goes up to him.*)

CHERRY: Please, can you take charge of the music for us?

> (JOHNNY *looks at her. Then he shakes his head.*

(NASSER, *in drunken, ebullient mood, takes* OMAR *across the room to* ZAKI, *who is with* SALIM.)

ZAKI: (*Shaking hands with* OMAR) Omar, my boy.

(SALIM *moves away.*)

NASSER(*To* OMAR, *of* ZAKI) Help him (*To* ZAKI.) Now tell him, please.

ZAKI: Oh God, Omo, I've got these two damn laundrettes in your area. I need big advice on them.

(*We hear Omar's voice as we look at the party.*)

OMAR: I won't advise you. If the laundrettes are a trouble to you I'll pay you rent for them plus a percentage of the profits.

NASSER: How about it, Zaki? He'll run them with Johnny.

(*We see* TANIA *talking to two interested* PARKISTANI MEN *in their middle twenties who see her as marriageable and laugh at everything she says. But* TANIA *is looking at* JOHNNY *who is on his own, drinking. He also dances, bending his knees and doing an inconspicuous handjive. He smiles at* TANIA.

TANIA *goes across to* JOHNNY. *He whispers something in her ear. She leads* JOHNNY *by the hand out into the garden.*

BILQUIS *looks in fury at* NASSER, *blaming him for this. He turns away from her.*

ZAKI *is happily explaining to his wife about the deal with* OMAR.)

EXT. GARDEN. EVENING

TANIA *leads* JOHNNY *across the garden, towards the little garden house at the end. A bicycle is leaning against it. She takes off her shoes. And they hold each other and dance.*

INT. THE HOUSE. EVENING

SALIM *is on his own a moment.* OMAR *moves towards him.* SALIM *walks out and across the garden.*

EXT. GARDEN. EVENING

OMAR *follows* SALIM *across the lawn.*

OMAR: I've got it. (SALIM *turns to him.*) The instalment. It's hefty, Salim. More than you wanted.

(OMAR *fumbles for the money in his jacket pocket. At the end of the garden* JOHNNY *and* TANIA *are playing around with a bicycle.* OMAR, *shaking, drops some of the money.* SALIM *raises his hand in smiling rejection.*)

SALIM: Don't ever offer me money. It was an educational test I put on you. To make you see you did a wrong thing.

(TANIA *and* JOHNNY *are now riding the bicycle on the lawn.*) Don't in future bite the family hand when you can eat out of it. If you need money just ask me. Years ago your uncles lifted me up. And I will do the same for you.

(*Through this* OMAR *has become increasingly concerned as* TANIA, *with* JOHNNY *on the back of the bicycle, is riding at Salim's back.* OMAR *shouts out.*)

OMAR: Tania!

(*And he tries to pull* SALIM *out of the way. But* TANIA *crashes into* SALIM, *knocking him flying flat on his face.* NASSER *comes rushing down the lawn.*

TANIA *and* JOHNNY *lie laughing on their backs.*

SALIM *gets up quickly, furiously, and goes to punch* JOHNNY. OMAR *and* NASSER *grab an arm of* SALIM's *each.* JOHNNY *laughs in* SALIM's *face.*)

(*To* SALIM) All right, all right, he's no one.

(SALIM *calms down quickly and just raises a warning finger at* JOHNNY. *The confrontation is mainly diverted by* NASSER *going for* TANIA.)

NASSER: (*To* TANIA) You little bitch! (*He grabs at* TANIA *to hit her.* JOHNNY *pulls her away.*) What the hell d'you think you're doing?

SALIM: (*To* NASSER) Can't you control your bloody people?

(*And he abuses* NASSER *in Urdu.* NASSER *curses and scowls in English:*) Why should you be able to? You've gambled most of your money down the toilet! (SALIM *turns and walks away.*)

TANIA: (*Pointing after him*) That smooth suppository owns us! Everything! Our education, your businesses, Rachel's stockings. It's his!

NASSER: (*To* OMAR) Aren't you two getting married?

OMAR: Yes, yes, any day now.

TANIA: I'd rather drink my own urine.

OMAR: I hear it can be quite tasty, with a slice of lemon.

NASSER: Get out of my sight, Tania!

TANIA: I'm going further than that.

(NASSER *turns and storms away. As he walks up the lawn we see that* BILQUIS *has been standing a quarter of the way down the lawn, witnessing all this.*

NASSER *stops for a moment beside her, not looking at her. He walks on.*)

OMAR: (*To* JOHNNY) Let's get out of here.

TANIA: (*To* JOHNNY) Take me.

(OMAR *shakes his head and takes* JOHNNY*'s hand.*)

OMAR: Salim'll give us a lift.

JOHNNY: What?

OMAR: I need him for something I've got in mind.

INT. SALIM'S CAR. NIGHT

SALIM *is driving* JOHNNY *and* OMAR *along a country lane, fast, away from Nasser's house.*

JOHNNY *is sitting in the back, looking out of the window.*

OMAR *is sarcastic for* JOHNNY*'s unheeding benefit and undetected by the humourless* SALIM.

OMAR: Well, thanks, Salim, you know. For saving the laundrette and everything. And for giving us a lift. Our car's bust.

SALIM: (*Accelerating*) Got to get to a little liaison. (*To* JOHNNY.) He doesn't have to thank me. Eh, Johnny? What's your problem with me, Johnny?

JOHNNY: (*Eventually, and tough*) Salim, we know what you sell, man. Know the kids you sell it to. It's shit, man. Shit.

SALIM: Haven't you noticed? People are shit. I give them what they want. I don't criticize. I supply. The laws of business apply.

JOHNNY: Christ, what a view of people. Eh, Omo? You think that's a filthy shit thing, don't you, Omo?

(*Suddenly* SALIM *steps on the brakes. They skid to a stop on the edge of a steep drop away from the road.*)

SALIM: Get out!

(JOHNNY *opens the car door. He looks down the steep hill and across the windy Kent landscape. He leans back in his seat, closing the car door.*)

JOHNNY: I don't like the country. The snakes make me nervous.
(SALIM *laughs and drives off.*)

INT. SALIM'S CAR. NIGHT
They've reached South London, near the laundrette.
    OMAR*'s been explaining to* SALIM *about his new scheme.*
OMAR: . . . So I was talking to Zaki about it. I want to take over
    his two laundrettes. He's got no idea.
SALIM: None.
OMAR: Do them up. With this money. (*He pats his pocket.*)
SALIM: Yeah. Is it enough?
OMAR: I thought maybe you could come in with me . . .
    financially.
SALIM: Yeah. I'm looking for some straight outlets. (*Pause.*)
    You're a smart bastard. (*Suddenly.*) Hey, hey, hey . . .
    (*And he sees, in the semi-darkness near the football ground, a
    group of roaming laughing* LADS. *They are walking into a
    narrow lane.* SALIM *slows the car down and enters the street
    behind them, following them now, watching them and
    explaining. To* JOHNNY.) These people. What a waste of
    life. They're filthy and ignorant. They're just nothing. But
    they abuse people. (*To* OMAR.) Our people. (*To* JOHNNY.)
    All over England, Asians, as you call us, are beaten, burnt
    to death. Always we are intimidated. What these scum
    need – (*and he slams the car into gear and starts to drive
    forward fast*)) is a taste of their own piss.
    (*He accelerates fast, and mounting the pavement, drives at the
    LADS ahead of him.* MOOSE *turns and sees the car. They scatter
    and run. Another of the* LADS *is* GENGHIS. *Some of the others
    we will recognize as mates of his.*
        GENGHIS *gets in close against the wall, picking up a lump of
    wood to smash through the car windscreen. But he doesn't have
    time to fling it and drops it as* SALIM *drives at him, turning
    away at the last minute.* GENGHIS *sees clearly who is in the
    front of the car.*
        As* SALIM *turns the car away from* GENGHIS, MOOSE *is
    suddenly standing stranded in the centre of the road.* SALIM
    can't avoid him. MOOSE *jumps aside but* SALIM *drives over his
    foot.* MOOSE *screams.*)

SALIM *drives on.*)

INT. JOHNNY'S ROOM. NIGHT

OMAR *and* JOHNNY *have made love.* OMAR *appears to be asleep, lying across the bed.*

JOHNNY *gets up, walks across the room and picks up a bottle of whisky. He drinks.*

INT. ANOTHER LAUNDRETTE. DAY

This is a much smaller and less splendid laundrette than Omar's.

OMAR *is looking it over 'expertly'.* ZAKI *is awaiting Omar's verdict. This is Zaki's problem laundrette.*

SALIM *is also there, striding moodily about.*

OMAR: I think I can do something with this. Me and my partner.

ZAKI: Take it. I trust you and your family.

OMAR: Salim?

SALIM: I'd happily put money into it.

OMAR: All right. Wait a minute.

EXT. OUTSIDE THIS SMALLER LAUNDRETTE. DAY

JOHNNY *is morosely sitting in the car, examining himself in the car mirror. In the mirror, at the far end of the street, he sees a figure on crutches watching them. This is* MOOSE.

OMAR *comes out of the laundrette and talks to* JOHNNY *through the car window.*

OMAR: You wanna look at this place? Think we could do something with it?

JOHNNY: Can't tell without seeing it.

OMAR: Come on, then.

JOHNNY: Not if that scum Salim's there.

(OMAR *turns away angrily and walks back into the laundrette.*)

EXT. OUTSIDE OMAR AND JOHNNY'S BEAUTIFUL LAUNDRETTE. DAY

GENGHIS *is standing on the roof of the laundrette, a plank of wood studded with nails in his hand.*

Across the street, in the alley and behind cars, the LADS *are waiting and watching the laundrette.* MOOSE *is with them, hobbling.*

Inside, JOHNNY *washes the floor.* TANIA, *not seeing* GENGHIS *or the* LADS, *walks down the street towards the laundrette.*

INT. LAUNDRETTE. DAY
JOHNNY *is washing the floor of the laundrette. A white* MAN *opens a washing machine and starts picking prawns out of it, putting them in a black plastic bag.* JOHNNY *watches in amazement.*

TANIA *comes into the laundrette to say goodbye to* JOHNNY. *She is carrying a bag.*

TANIA: (*Excited*) I'm going.
JOHNNY: Where?
TANIA: London. Away.
(*Some* KIDS *are playing football outside, dangerously near the laundrette windows.* JOHNNY *goes to the window and bangs on it. He spots a* LAD *and* MOOSE *watching the laundrette from across the street.* JOHNNY *waves at them. They ignore him.*)
(*To him*) I'm going, to live my life. You can come.
JOHNNY: No good jobs like this in London.
TANIA: Omo just runs you around everywhere like a servant.
JOHNNY: Well. I'll stay here with my friend and fight it out.
TANIA: My family, Salim and all, they'll swallow you up like a little kebab.
JOHNNY: I couldn't just leave him now. Don't ask me to. You ever touched him? (*She shakes her head.*) I wouldn't trust him, though.
TANIA: Better go. (*She kisses him and turns and goes. He stands at the door and watches her go.*)

EXT. OUTSIDE THE LAUNDRETTE. DAY
From the roof GENGHIS *watches* TANIA *walk away from the laundrette.*

At the end of the street, Salim's car turns the corner. A LAD *standing on the corner signals to* GENGHIS. GENGHIS *nods at the* LADS *in the alley opposite and holds his piece of wood ready.*

INT. CLUB/BAR. DAY
NASSER *and* RACHEL *are sitting at a table in the club/bar. They have been having an intense, terrible, sad conversation. Now they are staring at each other.* NASSER *holds her hand. She withdraws her hand.*

TARIQ *comes over to the table with two drinks. He puts them down. He wants to talk to* NASSER. NASSER *touches his arm, without looking up. And* TARIQ *goes.*

RACHEL: So . . . so . . . so that's it.

NASSER: Why? Why d'you have to leave me now? (*She shrugs.*) After all these days.

RACHEL: Years.

NASSER: Why say you're taking from my family?

RACHEL: Their love and money. Yes, apparently I am.

NASSER: No.

RACHEL: And it's not possible to enjoy being so hated.

NASSER: It'll stop.

RACHEL: Her work. (*She pulls up her jumper to reveal her blotched, marked stomach. If possible we should suspect for a moment that she is pregnant.*) And I am being cruel to her. It is impossible.

NASSER: Let me kiss you. (*She gets up.*) Oh, Christ. (*She turns to go.*) Oh, love. Don't go. Don't, Rachel. Don't go.

EXT. OUTSIDE LAUNDRETTE. DAY

SALIM *is sitting in his car outside the laundrette.* GENGHIS *stands above him on the roof, watching. Across the street the* LADS *wait in the alley, alert.*

SALIM *gets out of his car.*

EXT. OUTSIDE ANWAR'S CLUB. DAY

RACHEL *walks away from the club.* NASSER *stands at the door and watches her go.*

EXT. OUTSIDE PAPA'S HOUSE. DAY

NASSER *gets out of his car and walks towards Papa's house. The door is broken and he pushes it, going into the hall, to the bottom of the stairs.*

EXT. OUTSIDE THE LAUNDRETTE. DAY

SALIM *walks into the laundrette.*

INT. PAPA'S HOUSE. DAY

NASSER *sadly climbs the filthy stairs of the house in which Papa's flat is.*

INT. LAUNDRETTE. DAY

SALIM *has come into the busy laundrette.* JOHNNY *is working.*

SALIM: I want to talk to Omo about business.

JOHNNY: I dunno where he is.

SALIM: Is it worth waiting?

JOHNNY: In my experience it's always worth waiting for Omo.

(*The* TELEPHONE CHARACTER *is yelling into the receiver.*)

TELEPHONE CHARACTER: No, no, I promise I'll look after it. I
     want a child, don't I? Right, I'm coming round now! (*He
     slams the receiver down. Then he starts to dial again.*)

INT. PAPA'S HOUSE. DAY

NASSER *has reached the top of the stairs and the door to Papa's flat.
He opens the door with his key. He walks along the hall to Papa's
room. He stops at the open door to Papa's room.* PAPA *is lying in bed
completely still.* NASSER *looks at him, worried.*

EXT. OUTSIDE THE LAUNDRETTE. DAY

The LADS *are waiting in the alley opposite.* GENGHIS *gives them a
signal from the roof.*

     The LADS *run across the street and start to smash up Salim's car
with big sticks, laying into the headlights, the windscreen, the roof,
etc.*

INT. LAUNDRETTE. DAY

We are looking at the TELEPHONE CHARACTER. *He is holding the
receiver in one hand. His other hand over his mouth.* SALIM *sees him
and then turns to see, out of the laundrette window, his car being
demolished.*

INT. PAPA'S ROOM. DAY

NASSER *walks into Papa's room.* PAPA *hears him and looks up.*
PAPA *struggles to get to the edge of the bed, and thrusts himself into
the air.*

     NASSER *goes towards him and they embrace warmly, fervently.
Then* NASSER *sits down on the bed next to his brother.*

EXT. OUTSIDE THE LAUNDRETTE. DAY

SALIM *runs out of the laundrette towards his car. He grabs one of the*

LADS *and smashes the* LAD*'s head on the side of the car.*
GENGHIS *is standing above them, on the edge of the roof.*
GENGHIS: (*Yells*) Hey! Paki! Hey! Paki!

INT. PAPA'S ROOM. DAY
PAPA *and* NASSER *sit side by side on the bed.*
PAPA: This damn country has done us in. That's why I am like this. We should be there. Home.
NASSER: But that country has been sodomized by religion. It is beginning to interfere with the making of money.
Compared with everywhere, it is a little heaven here.

EXT. OUTSIDE THE LAUNDRETTE. DAY
SALIM *looks up at* GENGHIS *standing on the edge of the roof.*
Suddenly GENGHIS *jumps down, on top of* SALIM, *pulling* SALIM *to the ground with him.*
GENGHIS *quickly gets to his feet. And as* SALIM *gets up,*
GENGHIS *hits him across the face with the studded piece of wood, tearing* SALIM*'s face.*
JOHNNY *is watching from inside the laundrette.*

INT. PAPA'S ROOM. DAY
PAPA *and* NASSER *are sitting on the bed.*
PAPA: Why are you unhappy?
NASSER: Rachel has left me. I don't know what I'm going to do.
(*He gets up and goes to the door of the balcony.*)

EXT. OUTSIDE THE LAUNDRETTE. DAY
SALIM, *streaming blood, rushes at* GENGHIS. GENGHIS *smashes him in the stomach with the piece of wood.*

EXT. SOUTH LONDON STREET. DAY
OMAR *and* ZAKI *are walking along a South London street, away from Zaki's small laundrette.*
Across the street is the club/bar. TARIQ *is just coming out. He waves at* OMAR.
ZAKI: So you're planning an armada of laundrettes?
OMAR: What do you think of the dry-cleaners?
ZAKI: They are the past. But then they are the present also.

Mostly they are the past. But they are going to be the
future too, don't you think?

EXT. OUTSIDE THE LAUNDRETTE. DAY
SALIM *is on the ground.* MOOSE *goes to him and whacks him with
his crutch.* SALIM *lies still.* GENGHIS *kicks* SALIM *in the back. He is
about to kick him again.*
    JOHNNY *is standing at the door of the laundrette. He moves
towards* GENGHIS.
JOHNNY: He'll die.
    (GENGHIS *kicks* SALIM *again.* JOHNNY *loses his temper, rushes
    at* GENGHIS *and pushes him up against the car.*)
    I said: leave it out!
    (*One of the* LADS *moves towards* JOHNNY. GENGHIS *shakes
    his head at the* LAD. SALIM *starts to pull himself up off the
    floor.* JOHNNY *holds* GENGHIS *like a lover. To* SALIM.) Get
    out of here!
    (GENGHIS *punches* JOHNNY *in the stomach.* GENGHIS *and*
    JOHNNY *start to fight.* GENGHIS *is strong but* JOHNNY *is quick.*
    JOHNNY *tries twice to stop the fight, pulling away from* GENGHIS.)
    All right, let's leave it out now, eh?
    (SALIM *crawls away,* GENGHIS *hits* JOHNNY *very hard and*
    JOHNNY *goes down.*)

EXT. STREET. DAY
ZAKI *and* OMAR *turn the corner, into the street where the fight is
taking place.* ZAKI *sees* SALIM *staggering up the other side of the
street.* ZAKI *goes to him.*
    OMAR *runs towards the fight.* JOHNNY *is being badly beaten now.
A* LAD *grabs* OMAR. OMAR *struggles.*
    Suddenly the sound of police sirens. The fight scatters. As it does,
GENGHIS *throws his lump of wood through the laundrette window,
showering glass over the punters gathered round the window.*
    OMAR *goes to* JOHNNY, *who is barely conscious.*

EXT. BALCONY OF PAPA'S FLAT. DAY
NASSER *is standing leaning over the balcony, looking across the
railway track.* PAPA *comes through the balcony door and stands
behind him, in his pyjamas.*

NASSER: You still look after me, eh? But I'm finished.

PAPA: Only Omo matters.

NASSER: I'll make sure he's fixed up with a good business future.

PAPA: And marriage?

NASSER: Tania is a possibility?

(NASSER *nods confidently, perhaps over-confidently.*)

INT. BACK ROOM OF LAUNDRETTE. DAY

OMAR *is bathing* JOHNNY*'s badly bashed up face at the sink in the back room of the laundrette.*

OMAR: All right?

JOHNNY: What d'you mean all right? How can I be all right? I'm in the state I'm in. (*Pause.*) I'll be handsome. But where exactly am I?

OMAR: Where you should be. With me.

JOHNNY: No. Where does all this leave me?

OMAR: Are you crying?

JOHNNY: Where does it? Kiss me then.

OMAR: Don't cry. Your hand hurts too. That's why.

JOHNNY: Hey.

OMAR: What?

JOHNNY: I better go. I think I had, yeah.

OMAR: You were always going, at school. Always running about, you. Your hand is bad. I couldn't pin you down then.

JOHNNY: And now I'm going again. Give me my hand back.

OMAR: You're dirty. You're beautiful.

JOHNNY: I'm serious. Don't keep touching me.

OMAR: I'm going to give you a wash.

JOHNNY: You don't listen to anything.

OMAR: I'm filling this sink.

JOHNNY: Don't.

OMAR: Get over here! (OMAR *fills the sink.* JOHNNY *turns and goes out of the room.*) Johnny.

(*We follow* JOHNNY *out through the laundrette.*)

EXT. THE BALCONY. DAY

PAPA *turns away from* NASSER.

A train is approaching, rushing towards NASSER. *Suddenly it is passing him and for a moment, if this is technically possible, he sees* TANIA *sitting reading in the train, her bag beside her. He cries out, but he is drowned out by the train.*

If it is not possible for him to see her, then we go into the train with her and perhaps from her POV in the train look at the balcony, the two figures, at the back view of the flat passing by.

INT. LAUNDRETTE. DAY
JOHNNY *has got to the door of the laundrette.* OMAR *has rushed to the door of the back room.*

The shattered glass from the window is still all over the floor. A cold wind blows through the half-lit laundrette.

JOHNNY *stops at the door of the laundrette. He turns towards* OMAR.

INT. BACK ROOM OF LAUNDRETTE. DAY
As the film finishes, as the credits roll, OMAR *and* JOHNNY *are washing and splashing each other in the sink in the back room of the laundrette, both stripped to the waist. Music over this.*

The Rainbow Sign

'God gave Noah the rainbow sign,
No more water, the fire next time!'

ONE: ENGLAND

I was born in London of an English mother and Pakistani father. My father, who lives in London, came to England from Bombay in 1947 to be educated by the old colonial power. He married here and never went back to India. The rest of his large family, his brothers, their wives, his sisters, moved from Bombay to Karachi, in Pakistan, after partition.

Frequently during my childhood, I met my Pakistani uncles when they came to London on business. They were important, confident people who took me to hotels, restaurants and Test matches, often in taxis. But I had no idea of what the subcontinent was like or how my numerous uncles, aunts and cousins lived there. When I was nine or ten a teacher purposefully placed some pictures of Indian peasants in mud huts in front of me and said to the class: Hanif comes from India. I wondered: did my uncles ride on camels? Surely not in their suits? Did my cousins, so like me in other ways, squat down in the sand like little Mowglis, half-naked and eating with their fingers?

In the mid-1960s, Pakistanis were a risible subject in England, derided on television and exploited by politicians. They had the worst jobs, they were uncomfortable in England, some of them had difficulties with the language. They were despised and out of place.

From the start I tried to deny my Pakistani self. I was ashamed. It was a curse and I wanted to be rid of it. I wanted to be like everyone else. I read with understanding a story in a newspaper about a black boy who, when he noticed that burnt skin turned white, jumped into a bath of boiling water.

At school, one teacher always spoke to me in a 'Peter Sellers' Indian accent. Another refused to call me by my name, calling me Pakistani Pete instead. So I refused to call the teacher by *his* name and used his nickname instead. This led to trouble; arguments, detentions, escapes from school over hedges, and eventually suspension. This played into my hands; this couldn't have been better.

With a friend I roamed the streets and fields all day; I sat beside streams; I stole yellow lurex trousers from a shop and smuggled them out of the house under my school trousers; I hid in woods reading hard books; and I saw the film *Zulu* several times.

This friend, who became Johnny in my film, *My Beautiful Laundrette*, came one day to the house. It was a shock.

He was dressed in jeans so tough they almost stood up by themselves. These were suspended above his boots by Union Jack braces of 'hangman's strength', revealing a stretch of milk bottle white leg. He seemed to have sprung up several inches because of his Doctor Marten's boots, which had steel caps and soles as thick as cheese sandwiches. His Ben Sherman shirt with a pleat down the back was essential. And his hair, which was only a quarter of an inch long all over, stuck out of his head like little nails. This unmoving creation he concentratedly touched up every hour with a sharpened steel comb that also served as a dagger.

He soon got the name Bog Brush, though this was not a moniker you would use to his face. Where before he was an angel-boy with a blond quiff flattened down by his mother's loving spit, a clean handkerchief always in his pocket, as well as being a keen cornet player for the Air Cadets he'd now gained a brand-new truculent demeanour.

My mother was so terrified by this stormtrooper dancing on her doorstep to the 'Skinhead Moonstomp', which he moaned to himself continuously, that she had to lie down.

I decided to go out roaming with B.B. before my father got home from work. But it wasn't the same as before. We couldn't have our talks without being interrupted. Bog Brush had become Someone. To his intense pleasure, similarly dressed strangers greeted Bog Brush in the street as if they were in a war-torn foreign country and in the same army battalion. We were suddenly banned from cinemas. The Wimpy Bar in which we sat for hours with milkshakes wouldn't let us in. As a matter of pride we now had to go round the back and lob a brick at the rear window of the place.

Other strangers would spot us from the other side of the street. B.B. would yell 'Leg it!' as the enemy dashed through traffic and leapt over the bonnets of cars to get at us, screaming obscenities and chasing us up alleys, across allotments, around reservoirs, and on and on.

And then, in the evening, B.B. took me to meet with the other lads. We climbed the park railings and strolled across to the football pitch, by the goal posts. This is where the lads congregated to hunt down Pakistanis and beat them. Most of them I was at school with. The others I'd grown up with. I knew their parents. They knew my father.

I withdrew, from the park, from the lads, to a safer place, within myself. I moved into what I call my 'temporary' period. I was only waiting now to get away, to leave the London suburbs, to make another kind of life, somewhere else, with better people.

In this isolation, in my bedroom where I listened to the Pink Floyd, the Beatles and the John Peel Show, I started to write down the speeches of politicians, the words which helped create the neo-Nazi attitudes I saw around me. This I called 'keeping the accounts'.

In 1965, Enoch Powell said: 'We should not lose sight of the desirability of achieving a steady flow of voluntary repatriation for the elements which are proving unsuccessful or unassimilable.'

In 1967, Duncan Sandys said: 'The breeding of millions of half-caste children would merely produce a generation of misfits and create national tensions.'

I wasn't a misfit; I could join the elements of myself together. It was the others, they wanted misfits; they wanted you to embody within yourself their ambivalence.

Also in 1967, Enoch Powell – who once said he would love to have been Viceroy of India – quoted a constituent of his as saying that because of the Pakistanis 'this country will not be worth living in for our children'.

And Powell said, more famously: 'As I look ahead I am filled with foreboding. Like the Roman, "I seem to see the River Tiber foaming with much blood".'

As Powell's speeches appeared in the papers, graffiti in support of him appeared in the London streets. Racists gained confidence. People insulted me in the street. Someone in a café refused to eat at the same table with me. The parents of a girl I was in love with told her she'd get a bad reputation by going out with darkies.

Powell allowed himself to become a figurehead for racists. He helped create racism in Britain and was directly responsible not only for the atmosphere of fear and hatred, but through his influence, for individual acts of violence against Pakistanis.

Television comics used Pakistanis as the butt of their humour. Their jokes were highly political: they contributed to a way of seeing the world. The enjoyed reduction of racial hatred to a joke did two things: it expressed a collective view (which was sanctioned by its being on the BBC), and it was a celebration of contempt in millions of living rooms in England. I was afraid to watch TV because of it; it was too embarrassing, too degrading.

Parents of my friends, both lower-middle-class and working-class, often told me they were Powell supporters. Sometimes I heard them talking, heatedly, violently, about race, about 'the Pakis'. I was desperately embarrassed and afraid of being identified with these loathed aliens. I found it almost impossible to answer questions about where I came from. The word 'Pakistani' had been made into an insult. It was a word I didn't want used about myself. I couldn't tolerate being myself.

The British complained incessantly that the Pakistanis wouldn't assimilate. This meant they wanted the Pakistanis to be exactly like them. But of course even then they would have rejected them.

The British were doing the assimilating: they assimilated Pakistanis to their world view. They saw them as dirty, ignorant and less than human – worthy of abuse and violence.

At this time I found it difficult to get along with anyone. I was frightened and hostile. I suspected that my white friends were capable of racist insults. And many of them did taunt me, innocently. I reckoned that at least once every day since I was five years old I had been racially abused. I became incapable of distinguishing between remarks that were genuinely intended to hurt and those intended as 'humour'.

I became cold and distant. I began to feel I was very violent. But I didn't know how to be violent. If I had known, if that had come naturally to me, or if there'd been others I could follow, I would have made my constant fantasies of revenge into realities,

I would have got into trouble, willingly hurt people, or set fire to things.

But I mooched around libraries. There, in an old copy of *Life* magazine, I found pictures of the Black Panthers. It was Eldridge Cleaver, Huey Newton, Bobby Seale and their confederates in black vests and slacks, with Jimi Hendrix haircuts. Some of them were holding guns, the Army .45 and the 12-gauge Magnum shotgun with 18-inch barrel that Huey specified for street fighting.

I tore down my pictures of the Rolling Stones and Cream and replaced them with the Panthers. I found it all exhilarating. These people were proud and they were fighting. To my knowledge, no one in England was fighting.

There was another, more important picture.

On the cover of the Penguin edition of *The Fire Next Time*, was James Baldwin holding a child, his nephew. Baldwin, having suffered, having been there, was all anger and understanding. He was intelligence and love combined. As I planned my escape I read Baldwin all the time, I read Richard Wright and I admired Muhammad Ali.

A great moment occurred when I was in a sweet shop. I saw through to a TV in the backroom on which was showing the 1968 Olympic Games in Mexico. Thommie Smith and John Carlos were raising their fists on the victory rostrum, giving the Black Power salute as the 'Star Spangled Banner' played. The white shopkeeper was outraged. He said to me: they shouldn't mix politics and sport.

During this time there was always Muhammad Ali, the former Cassius Clay, a great sportsman become black spokesman. Now a Muslim, millions of fellow Muslims all over the world prayed for his victory when he fought.

And there was the Nation of Islam movement to which Ali belonged, led by the man who called himself the Messenger of Islam and wore a gold-embroidered fez, Elijah Muhammad.

Elijah was saying in the mid-1960s that the rule of the white devils would end in fifteen years. He preached separatism, separate development for black and white. He ran his organization by charisma and threat, claiming that anyone who challenged him would be chastened by Allah. Apparently Allah also turned the minds of defectors into a turmoil.

Elijah's disciple Malcolm X, admirer of Gandhi and self-confirmed anti-Semite, accepted in prison that 'the key to a Muslim is submission, the attunement of one towards Allah'. That this glorious resistance to the white man, the dismissal of Christian meekness, was followed by submission to Allah and worse, to Elijah Muhammad, was difficult to take.

I saw racism as unreason and prejudice, ignorance and a failure of sense; it was Fanon's 'incomprehension'. That the men I wanted to admire had liberated themselves only to take to unreason, to the abdication of intelligence, was shocking to me. And the separatism, the total loathing of the white man as innately corrupt, the 'All whites are devils' view, was equally unacceptable. I had to live in England, in the suburbs of London, with whites. My mother was white. I wasn't ready for separate development. I'd had too much of that already.

Luckily James Baldwin wasn't too keen either. In *The Fire Next Time* he describes a visit to Elijah Muhammed. He tells of how close he feels to Elijah and how he wishes to be able to love him. But when he tells Elijah that he has many white friends, he receives Elijah's pity. For Elijah the whites' time is up. It's no good Baldwin telling him he has white friends with whom he'd entrust his life.

As the evening goes on, Baldwin tires of the sycophancy around Elijah. He and Elijah would always be strangers and 'possibly enemies'. Baldwin deplores the black Muslims' turning to Africa and to Islam, this turning away from the reality of America and 'inventing' the past. Baldwin also mentions Malcolm X and the chief of the American Nazi party saying that racially speaking they were in complete agreement: they both wanted separate development. Baldwin adds that the debasement of one race and the glorification of another in this way inevitably leads to murder.

After this the Muslims weren't too keen on Baldwin, to say the least. Eldridge Cleaver, who once raped white women 'on principle', had a picture of Elijah Muhammad, the great strength-giver, on his prison wall. Later he became a devoted supporter of Malcolm X.

Cleaver says of Baldwin: 'There is in James Baldwin's work

the most gruelling, agonizing, total hatred of the blacks, particularly of himself, and the most shameful, fanatical, fawning, sycophantic love of the white that one can find in the writing of any black American writer of note in our time.'

How strange it was to me, this worthless abuse of a writer who could enter the minds and skins of both black and white, and the good just anger turning to passionate Islam as a source of pride instead of to a digested political commitment to a different kind of whole society. And this easy thrilling talk of 'white devils' instead of close analysis of the institutions that kept blacks low.

I saw the taking up of Islam as an aberration, a desperate fantasy of world-wide black brotherhood; it was a symptom of extreme alienation. It was also an inability to seek a wider political view or cooperation with other oppressed groups – or with the working class as a whole – since alliance with white groups was necessarily out of the question.

I had no idea what an Islamic society would be like, what the application of the authoritarian theology Elijah preached would mean in practice. I forgot about it, fled the suburbs, went to university, got started as a writer and worked as an usher at the Royal Court Theatre. It was over ten years before I went to an Islamic country.

TWO: PAKISTAN

The man had heard that I was interested in talking about his country, Pakistan, and that this was my first visit. He kindly kept trying to take me aside to talk. But I was already being talked to.

I was at another Karachi party, in a huge house, with a glass of whisky in one hand, and a paper plate in the other. Casually I'd mentioned to a woman friend of the family that I wasn't against marriage. Now this friend was earnestly recommending to me a young woman who wanted to move to Britain, with a husband. To my discomfort this go-between was trying to fix a time for the three of us to meet and negotiate.

I went to three parties a week in Karachi. This time, when I could get away from this woman, I was with landowners, diplomats, businessmen and politicians: powerful people. This pleased me. They were people I wouldn't have been able to get to in England and I wanted to write about them.

They were drinking heavily. Every liberal in England knows you can be lashed for drinking in Pakistan. But as far as I could tell, none of this English-speaking international bourgeoisie would be lashed for anything. They all had their favourite trusted bootleggers who negotiated the potholes of Karachi at high speed on disintegrating motorcycles, with the hooch stashed on the back. Bad bootleggers passed a hot needle through the neck of your bottle and drew your whisky out. Stories were told of guests politely sipping ginger beer with their ice and soda, glancing at other guests to see if they were drunk and wondering if their own alcohol tolerance had miraculously increased.

I once walked into a host's bathroom to see the bath full of floating whisky bottles being soaked to remove the labels, a servant sitting on a stool serenely poking at them with a stick.

So it was all as tricky and expensive as buying cocaine in London, with the advantage that as the hooch market was so competitive, the 'leggers delivered video tapes at the same time, dashing into the room towards the TV with hot copies of *The Jewel In The Crown*, *The Far Pavilions*, and an especially popular programme called *Mind Your Language*, which represented Indians and Pakistanis as ludicrous caricatures.

Everyone, except the mass of the population, had videos. And I could see why, since Pakistan TV was so peculiar. On my first day I turned it on and a cricket match was taking place. I settled in my chair. But the English players, who were on tour in Pakistan, were leaving the pitch. In fact, Bob Willis and Ian Botham were running towards the dressing rooms surrounded by armed police and this wasn't because Botham had made derogatory remarks about Pakistan. (He said it was a country to which he'd like to send his mother-in-law.) In the background a section of the crowd was being tear-gassed. Then the screen went blank.

Stranger still, and more significant, was the fact that the news was now being read in Arabic, a language few people in Pakistan understood. Someone explained to me that this was because the Koran was in Arabic, but everyone else said it was because

General Zia wanted to kiss the arses of the Arabs.

The man at the party, who was drunk, wanted to tell me something and kept pulling at me. The man was worried. But wasn't I worried too? I was trapped with this woman and the marriage proposal.

I has having a little identity crisis. I'd been greeted so warmly in Pakistan, I felt so excited by what I saw, and so at home with all my uncles, I wondered if I were not better off here than there. And when I said, with a little unnoticed irony, that I was an Englishman, people laughed. They fell about. Why would anyone with a brown face, Muslim name and large well-known family in Pakistan want to lay claim to that cold little decrepit island off Europe where you always had to spell your name? Strangely, anti-British remarks made me feel patriotic, though I only felt patriotic when I was away from England.

But I couldn't allow myself to feel too Pakistani. I didn't want to give in to that falsity, that sentimentality. As someone said to me at a party, provoked by the fact I was wearing jeans: we are Pakistanis, but you, you will always be a Paki – emphasizing the slang derogatory name the English used against Pakistanis, and therefore the fact that I couldn't rightfully lay claim to either place.

In England I was a playwright. In Karachi this meant little. There were no theatres; the arts were discouraged by the state – music and dancing are un-Islamic – and ignored by practically everyone else. So despite everything I felt pretty out of place.

The automatic status I gained through my family obtained for me such acceptance, respect and luxury that for the first time I could understand the privileged and their penchant for marshalling ridiculous arguments to justify their delicious and untenable position as an élite. But as I wasn't a doctor, or businessman or military person, people suspected that this writing business I talked about was a complicated excuse for idleness, uselessness and general bumming around. In fact, as I proclaimed an interest in the entertainment business, and talked much and loudly about how integral the arts were to a society, moves were being made to set me up in the amusement arcade business, in Shepherd's Bush.

Finally the man got me on my own. His name was Rahman.

He was a friend of my intellectual uncle. I had many uncles, but Rahman preferred the intellectual one who understood Rahman's particular sorrow and like him considered himself to be a marginal man.

In his fifties, a former Air Force officer, Rahman was liberal, well-travelled and married to an Englishwoman who now had a Pakistani accent.

He said to me: 'I tell you, this country is being sodomized by religion. It is even beginning to interfere with the making of money. And now we are embarked on this dynamic regression, you must know, it is obvious, Pakistan has become a leading country to go away from. Our patriots are abroad. We despise and envy them. For the rest of us, our class, your family, we are in Hobbes's state of nature: insecure, frightened. We cling together out of necessity.' He became optimistic. 'We could be like Japan, a tragic oriental country that is now progressive, industrialized.' He laughed and then said, ambiguously: 'But only God keeps this country together. You must say this around the world: we are taking a great leap backwards.'

The bitterest blow for Rahman was the dancing. He liked to waltz and foxtrot. But now the expression of physical joy, of sensuality and rhythm, was banned. On TV you could see where it had been censored. When couples in Western programmes got up to dance there'd be a jerk in the film, and they'd be sitting down again. For Rahman it was inexplicable, an unnecessary cruelty that was almost more arbitrary than anything else.

Thus the despair of Rahman and my uncles' 'high and dry' generation. Mostly educated in Britain, like Jinnah, the founder of Pakistan – who was a smoking, drinking, non-Urdu speaking lawyer and claimed that Pakistan would never be a theocracy ('that Britisher' he was sometimes called) – their intellectual mentors were Tawney, Shaw, Russell, Laski. For them the new Islamization was the negation of their lives.

It was a lament I heard often. This was the story they told. Karachi was a goodish place in the 1960s and 1970s. Until about 1977 it was lively and vigorous. You could drink and dance in the Raj-style clubs (providing you were admitted) and the atmosphere was liberal – as long as you didn't meddle in politics, in which case you'd probably be imprisoned. Politically there was

Bhutto: urbane, Oxford-educated, considering himself to be a poet and revolutionary, a veritable Chairman Mao of the sub-continent. He said he would fight obscurantism and illiteracy, ensure the equality of men and women, and increase access to education and medical care. The desert would bloom.

Later, in an attempt to save himself, appease the mullahs and rouse the dissatisfied masses behind him, he introduced various Koranic injunctions into the constitution and banned alcohol, gambling, horse-racing. The Islamization had begun, and was fervently continued after his execution.

Islamization built no hospitals, no schools, no houses; it cleaned no water and installed no electricity. But it was direction, identity. The country was to be in the hands of the divine, or rather, in the hands of those who elected themselves to interpret the single divine purpose. Under the tyranny of the priesthood, with the cooperation of the army, Pakistan would embody Islam in itself.

There would now be no distinction between ethical and religious obligation; there would now be no areas in which it was possible to be wrong. The only possible incertitude was of interpretation. The theory would be the written eternal and universal principles which Allah created and made obligatory for men; the model would be the first three generations of Muslims; and the practice would be Pakistan.

As a Professor of Law at the Islamic University wrote: 'Pakistan accepts Islam as the basis of economic and political life. We do not have a single reason to make any separation between Islam and Pakistan society. Pakistanis now adhere rigorously to Islam and cling steadfastly to their religious heritage. They never speak of these things with disrespect. With an acceleration in the process of Islamization, governmental capabilities increase and national identity and loyalty become stronger. Because Islamic civilization has brought Pakistanis very close to certainty, this society is ideally imbued with a moral mission.'

This moral mission and the over-emphasis on dogma and punishment, resulted in the kind of strengthening of the repressive, militaristic and nationalistically aggressive state seen all over the world in the authoritarian 1980s. With the added bonus that in Pakistan, God was always on the side of the government.

But despite all the strident nationalism, as Rahman said, the patriots were abroad; people were going away: to the West, to Saudi Arabia, anywhere. Young people continually asked me about the possibility of getting into Britain and some thought of taking some smack with them to bankroll their establishment. They had what was called the Gulf Syndrome, a condition I recognized from my time living in the suburbs. It was a dangerous psychological cocktail consisting of ambition, suppressed excitement, bitterness and sexual longing.

Then a disturbing incident occurred which seemed to encapsulate the going-away fever. An eighteen-year-old girl from a village called Chakwal dreamed that the villagers walked across the Arabian Sea to Karbala where they found money and work. Following this dream the village set off one night for the beach which happened to be near my uncle's house, in fashionable Clifton. Here lived politicians and diplomats in LA-style white bungalows with sprinklers on the lawn, a Mercedes in the drive and dogs and watchmen at the gates.

Here Benazir Bhutto was under house arrest. Her dead father's mansion was patrolled by the army who boredly nursed machine-guns and sat in tents beneath the high walls.

On the beach, the site of barbecues and late-night parties, the men of the Chakwal village packed the women and children into trunks and pushed them into the Arabian Sea. Then they followed them into the water, in the direction of Karbala. All but twenty of the potential *émigrés* were drowned. The survivors were arrested and charged with illegal emigration.

It was the talk of Karachi. It caused much amusement but people like Rahman despaired of a society that could be so confused, so advanced in some respects, so very naïve in others.

And all the (more orthodox) going away disturbed and confused the family set-up. When the men who'd been away came back, they were different, they were dissatisfied, they had seen more, they wanted more. Their neighbours were envious and resentful. Once more the society was being changed by outside forces, not by its own volition.

About twelve people lived permanently in my uncle's house,

plus servants who slept in sheds at the back, just behind the chickens and dogs. Relatives sometimes came to stay for months. New bits had to be built on to the house. All day there were visitors; in the evenings crowds of people came over; they were welcome, and they ate and watched videos and talked for hours. People weren't so protective of their privacy as they were in London.

This made me think about the close-bonding within the families and about the intimacy and interference of an extended family and a more public way of life. Was the extended family worse than the little nuclear family because there were more people to dislike? Or better because relationships were less intense?

Strangely, bourgeois-bohemian life in London, in Notting Hill and Islington and Fulham, was far more formal. It was frozen dinner parties and the division of social life into the meeting of couples with other couples, to discuss the lives of other coupling couples. Months would pass, then this would happen again.

In Pakistan, there was the continuity of the various families' knowledge of each other. People were easy to place; your grandparents and theirs were friends. When I went to the bank and showed the teller my passport, it turned out he knew several of my uncles, so I didn't receive the usual perfunctory treatment. This was how things worked.

I compared the collective hierarchy of the family and the performance of my family's circle, with my feckless, rather rootless life in London, in what was called 'the inner city'. There I lived alone, and lacked any long connection with anything. I'd hardly known anyone for more than eight years, and certainly not their parents. People came and went. There was much false intimacy and forced friendship. People didn't take responsibility for each other.

Many of my friends lived alone in London, especially the women. They wanted to be independent and to enter into relationships – as many as they liked, with whom they liked – out of choice. They didn't merely want to reproduce the old patterns of living. The future was to be determined by choice and reason, not by custom. The notions of duty and obligation barely had positive meaning for my friends; they were loaded, Victorian words, redolent of constraint and grandfather clocks, the antithesis of generosity in love, the new hugging, and the transcendence of the family. The ideal of the new relationship was no longer the S and M of the old marriage – it was F and C, freedom plus commitment.

In the large, old families where there was nothing but the old patterns, disturbed only occasionally by the new ways, this would have seemed a contrivance, a sort of immaturity, a failure to understand and accept the determinacies that life necessarily involved.

So there was much pressure to conform, especially on the women.

'Let these women be warned,' said a mullah to the dissenting women of Rawalpindi. 'We will tear them to pieces. We will give them such terrible punishments that no one in future will dare to raise a voice against Islam.'

I remember a woman saying to me at dinner one night: 'We know at least one thing. God will never dare to show his face in this country – the women will tear him apart!'

The family scrutiny and criticism was difficult to take, as was all the bitching and gossip. But there was warmth and continuity for a large number of people; there was security and much love. Also there was a sense of duty and community – of people's lives genuinely being lived together, whether they liked each other or not – that you didn't get in London. There, those who'd eschewed the family hadn't succeeded in creating some other form of supportive common life. In Pakistan there was that supportive common life, but at the expense of movement and change.

In the 1960s of Enoch Powell and graffiti, the Black Muslims and Malcolm X gave needed strength to the descendants of slaves by 'taking the wraps off the white man'; Eldridge Cleaver was yet to be converted to Christianity and Huey P. Newton was toting his Army .45. A boy in a bedroom in a suburb, who had the King's Road constantly on his mind and who changed the picture on his wall from week to week, was unhappy, and separated from the 1960s as by a thick glass wall against which he could only press his face. But bits of the 1960s were still around in Pakistan: the liberation rhetoric, for example, the music, the clothes, the drugs, not as the way of life they were originally intended to be, but as appendages to another, stronger tradition.

As my friends and I went into the Bara Market near Peshawar, close to the border of Afghanistan, in a rattling motorized rickshaw, I became apprehensive. There were large signs by the road telling foreigners that the police couldn't take responsibility for them: beyond this point the police would not go. Apparently the Pathans there, who were mostly refugees from Afghanistan, liked to kidnap foreigners and extort ransoms. My friends, who were keen to buy opium, which they'd give to the rickshaw driver to carry, told me everything was all right, because I wasn't a foreigner. I kept forgetting that.

The men were tough, martial, insular and proud. They lived in mud houses and tin shacks built like forts for shooting from. They were inevitably armed, with machine-guns slung over their shoulders. In the street you wouldn't believe women existed here, except you knew they took care of the legions of young men in the area who'd fled from Afghanistan to avoid being conscripted by the Russians and sent to Moscow for re-education.

Ankle deep in mud, I went round the market. Pistols, knives, Russian-made rifles, hand grenades and large lumps of dope and opium were laid out on stalls like tomatoes and oranges. Everyone was selling heroin.

The Americans, who had much money invested in Pakistan, in this compliant right-wing buffer-zone between Afghanistan and India, were furious that their children were being destroyed by a flourishing illegal industry in a country they financed. But the Americans sent to Pakistan could do little about it. Involvement in the heroin trade went right through Pakistan society: the police, the judiciary, the army, the landlords, the customs officials were all involved. After all, there was nothing in the Koran about heroin, nothing specific. I was even told that its export made ideological sense. Heroin was anti-Western; addiction in Western children was a deserved symptom of the moral vertigo of godless societies. It was a kind of colonial revenge. Reverse imperialism, the Karachi wits called it, inviting nemesis. The reverse imperialism was itself being reversed.

87

In a flat high above Karachi, an eighteen-year-old kid strung-out on heroin danced cheerfully around the room in front of me and pointed to an erection in the front of his trousers, which he referred to as his Imran Khan, the name of the handsome Pakistan cricket captain. More and more of the so-called multinational kids were taking heroin now. My friends who owned the flat, journalists on a weekly paper, were embarrassed.

But they always had dope to offer their friends. These laid-back people were mostly professionals: lawyers, an inspector in the police who smoked what he confiscated, a newspaper magnate, and various other journalists. Heaven it was to smoke at midnight on the beach, as local fishermen, squatting respectfully behind you, fixed fat joints; and the 'erotic politicians' themselves, the Doors, played from a portable stereo while the Arabian Sea rolled on to the beach. Oddly, since heroin and dope were both indigenous to the country, it took the West to make them popular in the East.

In so far as colonizers and colonized engage in a relationship with the latter aspiring to be like the former, you wouldn't catch anyone of my uncle's generation with a joint in their mouth. It was *infra dig* – for the peasants. Shadowing the British, they drank whisky and read *The Times*; they praised others by calling them 'gentlemen'; and their eyes filled with tears at old Vera Lynn records.

But the kids discussed yoga exercises. You'd catch them standing on their heads. They even meditated. Though one boy who worked at the airport said it was too much of a Hindu thing for Muslims to be doing; if his parents caught him chanting a mantra he'd get a backhander across the face. Mostly the kids listened to the Stones, Van Morrison and Bowie as they flew over ruined roads to the beach in bright red and yellow Japanese cars with quadrophonic speakers, past camels and acres of wasteland.

Here, all along the railway track, the poor and diseased and hungry lived in shacks and huts; the filthy poor gathered around rusty stand-pipes to fetch water; or ingeniously they resurrected wrecked cars, usually Morris Minors; and here they slept in huge sewer pipes among buffalo, chickens and wild dogs. Here I met a policeman who I thought was on duty. But the policeman lived

88

here, and hanging on the wall of his falling-down shed was his spare white police uniform, which he'd had to buy himself.

If not to the beach, the kids went to the Happy Hamburger to hang out. Or to each other's houses to watch Clint Eastwood tapes and giggle about sex, of which they were so ignorant and deprived. I watched a group of agitated young men in their mid-twenties gather around a 1950s' medical book to look at the female genitalia. For these boys, who watched Western films and mouthed the lyrics of pop songs celebrating desire ('come on, baby, light my fire'), life before marriage could only be like spending years and years in a single-sex public school; for them women were mysterious, unknown, desirable and yet threatening creatures of almost another species, whom you had to respect, marry and impregnate but couldn't be friends with. And in this country where the sexes were usually strictly segregated, the sexual tension could be palpable. The men who could afford to, flew to Bangkok for relief. The others squirmed and resented women. The kind of sexual openness that was one of the few real achievements of the 1960s, the discussion of contraception, abortion, female sexuality and prostitution which some women were trying to advance received incredible hostility. But women felt it was only a matter of time before progress was made; it was much harder to return to ignorance than the mullahs thought.

A stout intense lawyer in his early thirties of immense extrovert charm – with him it was definitely the 1980s, not the 1960s. His father was a judge. He himself was intelligent, articulate and fiercely representative of the other 'new spirit' of Pakistan. He didn't drink, smoke or fuck. Out of choice. He prayed five times a day. He worked all the time. He was determined to be a good Muslim, since that was the whole point of the country existing at all. He wasn't indulgent, except religiously, and he lived in accordance with what he believed. I took to him immediately.

We had dinner in an expensive restaurant. It could have been in London or New York. The food was excellent, I said. The lawyer disagreed, with his mouth full, shaking his great head. It was definitely no good, it was definitely meretricious rubbish. But for ideological reasons only, I concluded, since he ate with relish. He was only in the restaurant because of me, he said.

There was better food in the villages; the new food in Pakistan was, frankly, a tribute to chemistry rather than cuisine. Only the masses had virtue, they knew how to live, how to eat. He told me that those desiccated others, the marginal men I associated with and liked so much, were a plague class with no values. Perhaps, he suggested, eating massively, this was why I liked them, being English. Their education, their intellectual snobbery, made them un-Islamic. They didn't understand the masses and they spoke in English to cut themselves off from the people. Didn't the best jobs go to those with a foreign education? He was tired of those Westernized elders denigrating their country and its religious nature. They'd been contaminated by the West, they didn't know their own country, and the sooner they got out and were beaten up by racists abroad the better.

The lawyer and I went out into the street. It was busy, the streets full of strolling people. There were dancing camels and a Pakistan trade exhibition. The lawyer strode through it all, yelling. The exhibition was full of Pakistan-made imitations of Western goods: bathrooms in chocolate and strawberry, TVs with stereos attached; fans, air-conditioners, heaters; and an arcade full of space-invaders. The lawyer got agitated.

These were Western things, of no use to the masses. The masses didn't have water, what would they do with strawberry bathrooms? The masses wanted Islam, not space-invaders or . . . or elections. Are elections a Western thing? I asked. Don't they have them in India too? No, they're a Western thing, the lawyer said. How could they be required under Islam? There need only be one party – the party of the righteous.

This energetic lawyer would have pleased and then disappointed Third World intellectuals and revolutionaries from an earlier era, people like Fanon and Guevara. This talk of liberation – at last the acknowledgement of the virtue of the toiling masses, the struggle against neo-colonialism, its bourgeois stooges, and American interference – the entire recognizable rhetoric of freedom and struggle, ends in the lawyer's mind with the country on its knees, at prayer. Having started to look for itself it finds itself . . . in the eighth century.

Islam and the masses. My numerous meetings with scholars, revisionists, liberals who wanted the Koran 'creatively' interpreted to make it compatible with modern science. The many medieval monologues of mullahs I'd listened to. So much talk, theory and Byzantine analysis.

I strode into a room in my uncle's house. Half-hidden by a curtain, on a verandah, was an aged woman servant wearing my cousin's old clothes, praying. I stopped and watched her. In the morning as I lay in bed, she swept the floor of my room with some twigs bound together. She was at least sixty. Now, on the shabby prayer mat, she was tiny and around her the universe was endless, immense, but God was above her. I felt she was acknowledging that which was larger than her, humbling herself before the infinite, knowing and feeling her own insignificance. It was a truthful moment, not empty ritual. I wished I could do it.

I went with the lawyer to the Mosque in Lahore, the largest in the world. I took off my shoes, padded across the immense courtyard with the other men – women were not allowed – and got on my knees. I banged my forehead on the marble floor. Beside me a man in a similar posture gave a world-consuming yawn. I waited but could not lose myself in prayer. I could only travesty the woman's prayer, to whom it had a world of meaning.

Perhaps she did want a society in which her particular moral and religious beliefs were mirrored, and no others, instead of some plural, liberal mélange; a society in which her own cast of mind, her customs, way of life and obedience to God were established with full legal and constituted authority. But it wasn't as if anyone had asked her.

In Pakistan, England just wouldn't go away. Despite the Lahore lawyer, despite everything, England was very much on the minds of Pakistanis. Relics of the Raj were everywhere: buildings, monuments, Oxford accents, libraries full of English books, and newspapers. Many Pakistanis had relatives in England; thousands of Pakistani families depended on money sent from England. Visiting a village, a man told me through an interpreter, that when his three grandchildren visited from Bradford, he had to hire an interpreter to speak to them. It was happening all the time – the closeness of the two societies, and the distance.

Although Pakistanis still wanted to escape to England, the old men in their clubs and the young eating their hamburgers took great pleasure in England's decline and decay. The great master was fallen. Now it was seen as strikebound, drug-ridden, riot-torn, inefficient, disunited, a society which had moved too suddenly from puritanism to hedonism and now loathed itself. And the Karachi wits liked to ask me when I thought the Americans would decide the British were ready for self-government.

Yet people like Rahman still clung to what they called British ideals, maintaining that it is a society's ideals, its conception of human progress, that define the level of its civilization. They regretted, under the Islamization, the repudiation of the values which they said were the only positive aspect of Britain's legacy to the sub-continent. These were: the idea of secular institutions based on reason, not revelation or scripture; the idea that there were no final solutions to human problems; and the idea that the health and vigour of a society was bound up with its ability to tolerate and express a plurality of views on all issues, and that these views would be welcomed.

But England as it is today, the ubiquity of racism and the suffering of Pakistanis because of it, was another, stranger subject. When I talked about it, the response was unexpected. Those who'd been to England often told of being insulted, or beaten up, or harassed at the airport. But even these people had attitudes similar to those who hadn't been there.

It was that the English misunderstood the Pakistanis because they saw only the poor people, those from the villages, the illiterates, the peasants, the Pakistanis who didn't know how to use toilets, how to eat with knives and forks because they were poor. If the British could only see *them*, the rich, the educated, the sophisticated, they wouldn't be so hostile. They'd know what civilized people the Pakistanis really were. And then they'd like them.

The implication was that the poor who'd emigrated to the West to escape the strangulation of the rich in Pakistan, deserved the racism they received in Britain because they really were contemptible. The Pakistani middle class shared the disdain of the British for the *émigré* working class and peasantry of Pakistan.

It was interesting to see that the British working class (and not only the working class, of course) used the same vocabulary of contempt about Pakistanis – the charges of ignorance, laziness, fecklessness, uncleanliness – that their own, British middle class used about them. And they weren't able to see the similarity.

Racism goes hand-in-hand with class inequality. Among other things, racism is a kind of snobbery, a desire to see oneself as superior culturally and economically, and a desire to actively experience and enjoy that superiority by hostility or violence. And when that superiority of class and culture is unsure or not acknowledged by the Other – as it would be acknowledged by the servant and master in class-stable Pakistan – but is in doubt, as with the British working class and Pakistanis in England, then it has to be demonstrated physically. Everyone knows where they stand then – the class inequality is displayed, just as any other snob demonstrates superiority by exhibiting wealth or learning or ancestry.

So some of the middle class of Pakistan, who also used the familiar vocabulary of contempt about their own poor (and, incidentally, about the British poor) couldn't understand when I explained that British racists weren't discriminating in their racial discrimination: they loathed all Pakistanis and kicked whoever was nearest. To the English all Pakistanis were the same; racists didn't ask whether you had a chauffeur, TV and private education before they set fire to your house. But for some Pakistanis, it was their own poor who had brought this upon them.

THREE: ENGLAND

It has been an arduous journey. Since Enoch Powell in the 1960s, there have been racist marches through South London approved by the Labour Home Secretary; attacks by busloads of racists on Southall, which the Asians violently and successfully repelled; and the complicated affair of young Asians burned to death and Asian shops razed to the ground by young blacks in Handsworth, Birmingham. The insults, the beatings, the murders continue. Although there has been white anger and various race relations legislation, Pakistanis are discriminated against in all areas.

Powell's awful prophecy was fulfilled: the hate he worked to create and the party of which he was a member, brought about his prediction. The River Tiber has indeed overflowed with much blood – Pakistani blood. And seventeen years later Powell has once more called for repatriation, giving succour to those who hate.

The fight back is under way. The defence committees, vigilante groups, study groups, trade union and women's groups are flourishing. People have changed, become united, through struggle and self-defence. My white friends, like Bog Brush, didn't enjoy fighting Pakistanis. They had a reputation for premature sobbing and cowardice. You didn't get your money's worth fighting a Paki. That's quite different now.

The fierce truculent pride of the Black Panthers is here now, as is the separatism, the violence, the bitterness and pathetic elevation of an imaginary homeland. This is directly spawned by racism.

Our cities are full of Asian shops. Where one would want black united with black, there are class differences as with all groups. Those Pakistanis who have worked hard to establish businesses, now vote Tory and give money to the Conservative Party. Their interests are the same as those of middle-class business people everywhere, though they are subject to more jealousy and violence. They have wanted to elevate themselves out of the maelstrom and by gaining economic power and the opportunity and dignity it brings, they have made themselves safe – safer. They have taken advantage of England.

But what is the Conservative view of them? Roger Scruton in his book *The Meaning Of Conservatism* sets out the case against mutual respect and understanding.

Firstly he deplores all race relations legislation and tries to justify certain kinds of racism by making it seem a harmless preference for certain kinds of people. He calls this preference a 'natural offshoot' of allegiance. Secondly, and more tellingly, he says that 'illiberal sentiments . . . arise inevitably from social consciousness: they involve natural prejudice, and a desire for the company of one's kind. That is hardly sufficient ground to condemn them as "racist".'

The crucial Conservative idea here is Scruton's notion of 'the company of one's kind'. What is the company of one's kind? Who exactly is of one's kind and what kind of people are they? Are they only those of the same 'nation', of the same colour, race and background? I suspect that that is what Scruton intends. But what a feeble, bloodless, narrow conception of human relationships and the possibilities of love and communication that he can only see 'one's kind' in this exclusive and complacent way!

One does seek the company of one's kind, of those in the same street, in the same club, in the same office. But the idea that these are the only people one can get along with or identify with, that one's humanity is such a held-back thing that it can't extend beyond this, leads to the denigration of those unlike onself. It leads to the idea that others have less humanity than oneself or one's own group or 'kind'; and to the idea of the Enemy, of the alien, of the Other. As Baldwin says: 'this inevitably leads to murder', and of course it has often done so in England recently.

Scruton quotes approvingly those who call this view 'death camp chic'. He would argue, I suppose, that loyalty and allegiance to one's kind doesn't necessarily lead to loathing of those not of one's kind. But Scruton himself talks of the 'alien wedge' and says that 'immigration cannot be an object of merely passive contemplation on the part of the present citizenship'.

The evil of racism is that it is a violation not only of another's dignity, but also of one's own person or soul; the failure of connection with others is a failure to understand or feel what it is one's own humanity consists in, what it is to be alive, and what it is to see both oneself and others as being ends not means, and as having souls. However much anodyne talk there is of 'one's kind', a society that is racist is a society that cannot accept itself, that hates parts of itself so deeply that it cannot see, does not want to see – because of its spiritual and political nullity and inanition – how much people have in common with each other. And the whole society and every element in it, is reduced and degraded because of it. This is why racism isn't a minor or sub-problem: it reflects on the whole and weighs the entire society in the balance.

Therefore, in the end, one's feeling for others, one's under-standing of their humanity cannot be anything to do with their being of 'one's kind' in the narrow way Scruton specifies. It can't be to do with others having any personal qualities at all. For paradoxically, as Simone Weil says: 'So far from its being his person, what is sacred in a human being is the impersonal in him. Everything which is impersonal in man is sacred, and nothing else.'

What of Labour?

The Pakistani working class is as unprotected politically as it has ever been. Despite various paternalistic efforts and an attempt at a kind of 'Raj decency', racism is the Trojan Horse within the Labour movement. The Labour Party has failed to show that it is serious about combating racism and serious in representing the black working class. There are few black councillors, few black parliamentary candidates, few blacks on the General Management Committees of constituency Labour Parties, no blacks on the NEC and so on, right through the Labour and trade union movement.

In my own ward and management committee, I have seen racist attitudes that would shame some Tories. People have stood up at Labour Party meetings I have attended and delivered racist diatribes. I have seen blacks discouraged from joining the Labour Party, and when they have joined, actively discouraged from canvassing in case they discouraged white racists from voting Labour.

The Labour Party wishes to be egalitarian and liberal on the race issue but knows that vast numbers of its voters are neither. The party is afraid – in some parts consciously and in other parts unconsciously – that blacks and black issues are a vote loser. If the Labour Party occasionally wishes blacks to serve it, it does not desire to serve blacks. Hence it acknowledges that thousands of its supporters are racist. It refuses to confront that.

Others in the party believe that racism is a sub-issue which has to be subordinate to the class issues of the time: housing, unemployment, education, maintenance of the social services and so on. They believe that winning elections and representing the mass of the working class in Parliament is more important than giving office or power to blacks. This is the choice it has made. This is the kind of party it is, and insofar as this is true, the Labour Party is a truly representative party, representing inequality and racism.

Coming back to England was harder than going. I had culture shock in reverse. Images of plenty yelled at me. England seemed to be overflowing with . . . things. Things from all over the world. Things and information. Information though, which couldn't bite through the profound insularity and indifference.

In Pakistan people were keen to know: not only about Asia and the Middle East, but about Europe and the United States. They sought out information about the whole world. They needed it. They ordered books from Europe, listened to international radio and chewed up visiting academics like pieces of orange.

In Britain today, among the middle class, thinking and argument are almost entirely taboo. The other taboo, replacing death in its unacceptability, is money. As our society has become more divided, the acknowledgement of that division – which is a financial division, a matter of economic power – is out of the question. So money is not discussed. It is taken for granted that you have it: that you have means of obtaining it: that you are reasonably well off and gain status and influence over others because of it.

Accompanying this financial silence, and shoring up both the social division and the taboo, is the prohibition on thought. The discussion of a serious subject to a conclusion using logic, evidence and counter-evidence is an unacceptable social embarrassment. It just isn't done to argue: it is thought to be the same as rowing. One has opinions in England, but they are formed in private and clung to in public despite everything, despite their often being quite wrong.

There is real defensiveness and insecurity, a Victorian fear of revealing so much as a genital of an idea, the nipple of a notion or the sex of a syllogism. Where sexual exhibitionism and the discussion of positions and emissions is fashionable, indeed orthodox, thinking and argument are avoided.

In Pakistan it was essential to have knowledge because political discussion was serious. It mattered what you thought.

People put chairs in a circle, sat down, and *talked*. What was said to each other was necessary. Intellectual dignity was maintained, earned anxiety was expressed; you weren't alone; ideas and feelings were shared. These things had to be said, even in low voices, because absolute silence was intolerable, absolute silence was the acceptance of isolation and division. It was a relief to argue, to exercise intelligence in a country where intelligence was in itself a weapon and a threat.

I will never forget the hospitality, warmth and generosity of the people of Pakistan; the flowers on the lawn of the Sind Club, the sprawling open houses, full of air and people and the smell of spices; the unbelievable brightness of the light shining through a dust haze; the woman walking perfectly straight-backed along a street with an iron balanced on her head; the open-air typists outside the law courts; butterflies as big as clock faces; the man who slept with a chicken in his bed; my uncle's library, bought in the 1940s in Cambridge, where he was taught by Russell – though when I opened the books after being given the library, they were rotten with worms, the pitted pages falling apart just as I stood there. And the way the men shake hands. This is worth going into.

First you offer them your hand and they grasp it. The clasped hands are slapped then with their spare hand as an affirmation of initial contact. This is, as it were, the soup. Now they pull you to them for the main course, the full embrace, the steak. As you look over their shoulder, your bodies thrust together, your heat intermingled, they crack you on the back at least three times with their open palm. These are not negligible taps, but good healthy whacks, demonstrating equality and openness. Depending on the nature of the friendship, these whacks could go on a considerable time and may debilitate the sick or weak. But they must be reciprocated. This done, they will let you move away from them, but still holding your right hand. You are considered fully, with affection overbrimming, as they regard all of you, as they seem to take in your entire being from top to toe, from inside to out. At last, after complete contact has been made, all possibility of concealment or inhibition banished, they carefully let go of your hand as if it were a delicate object. *That is a greeting.*

And there was the photograph of my father in my uncle's room, in which he must have been about the same age as me. A picture in a house that contained fragments of my past: a house full of stories, of Bombay, Delhi, China; of feuds, wrestling matches, adulteries, windows, broken with hands, card games, impossible loves, and magic spells. Stories to help me see my place in the world and give me a sense of the past which could go into making a life in the present and the future. This was surely part of the way I could understand myself. This knowledge, garnered in my mid-twenties, would help me form an image of myself: I'd take it back to England where I needed it to protect myself. And it would be with me in London and the suburbs, making me stronger.

When I considered staying in Pakistan to regain more of my past and complete myself with it, I had to think that that was impossible. Didn't I already miss too much of England? And wasn't I too impatient with the illiberalism and lack of possibility of Pakistan?

So there was always going to be the necessary return to England. I came home . . . to my country.

This is difficult to say. 'My country' isn't a notion that comes easily. It is still difficult to answer the question, where do you come from? I have never wanted to identify with England. When Enoch Powell spoke for England I turned away in final disgust. I would rather walk naked down the street than stand up for the National Anthem. The pain of that period of my life, in the mid-1960s, is with me still. And when I originally wrote this piece I put it in the third person: Hanif saw this, Hanif felt that, because of the difficulty of directly addressing myself to what I felt then, of not wanting to think about it again. And perhaps that is why I took to writing in the first place, to make strong feelings into weak feelings.

But despite all this, some kind of identification with England remains.

It is strange to go away to the land of your ancestors, to find out how much you have in common with people there, yet at the same time to realize how British you are, the extent to which, as Orwell says: 'the suet puddings and the red pillar boxes have entered into your soul'. It isn't *that* you wanted to find out. But it is part of what you do find out. And you find out what little choice you have in the matter of your background and where you belong. You look forward to getting back; you think often of England and what it means to you – and you think often of what it means to be British.

Two days after my return I took my washing to a laundrette and gave it to the attendant only to be told she didn't touch the clothes of foreigners: she didn't want me anywhere near her blasted laundrette. More seriously: I read in the paper that a Pakistani family in the East End had been fire-bombed. A child was killed. This, of course, happens frequently. It is the pig's head through the window, the spit in the face, the children with the initials of racist organizations tattooed into their skin with razor blades, as well as the more polite forms of hatred.

I was in a rage. I thought: who wants to be British anyway? Or as a black American writer said: who wants to be integrated into a burning house anyway?

And indeed I know Pakistanis and Indians born and brought up here who consider their position to be the result of a diaspora: they are in exile, awaiting return to a better place, where they belong, where they are welcome. And there this 'belonging' will be total. This will be home, and peace.

It is not difficult to see how much illusion and falsity there is in this view. How much disappointment and unhappiness might be involved in going 'home' only to see the extent to which you have been formed by England and the depth of attachment you feel to the place, despite everything.

It isn't surprising that some people believe in this idea of 'home'. The alternative to believing it is more conflict here; it is more self-hatred; it is the continual struggle against racism; it is the continual adjustment to life in Britain. And blacks in Britain know they have made more than enough adjustments.

So what is it to be British?

In his 1941 essay 'England Your England' Orwell says: 'the gentleness of the English civilisation is perhaps its most marked characteristic'. He calls the country 'a family with the wrong members in control' and talks of the 'soundness and homogeneity of England'.

Elsewhere he considers the Indian character. He explains the 'maniacal suspiciousness' which, agreeing, he claims, with E. M. Forster in *A Passage To India*, he calls 'the besetting Indian vice . . .' But he has the grace to acknowledge in his essay 'Not Counting Niggers' 'that the overwhelming bulk of the British proletariat [lives] . . . in Asia and Africa'.

But this is niggardly. The main object of his praise is British 'tolerance' and he writes of 'their gentle manners'. He also says that this aspect of England 'is continuous, it stretches into the future and the past, there is something in it that persists'.

But does it persist? If this version of England was true then, in the 1930s and 1940s, it is under pressure now. From the point of view of thousands of black people it just does not apply. It is completely without basis.

Obviously tolerance in a stable, confident wartime society with a massive Empire is quite different to tolerance in a disintegrating uncertain society during an economic depression. But surely this would be the test; this would be just the time for this much-advertised tolerance in the British soul to manifest itself as more than vanity and self-congratulation. But it has not. Under real continuous strain it has failed.

Tolerant, gentle British whites have no idea how little of this tolerance is experienced by blacks here. No idea of the violence, hostility and contempt directed against black people every day by state and individual alike in this land once described by Orwell as being not one of 'rubber truncheons' or 'Jew-baiters' but of 'flower-lovers' with 'mild knobbly faces'. But in parts of England the flower-lovers are all gone, the rubber truncheons and Jew-baiters are at large, and if any real contemporary content is to be given to Orwell's blind social patriotism, then clichés about 'tolerance' must be seriously examined for depth and weight of substantial content.

In the meantime it must be made clear that blacks don't require 'tolerance' in this particular condescending way. It isn't this particular paternal tyranny that is wanted, since it is major adjustments to British society that have to be made.

I stress that it is the British who have to make these adjustments.

It is the British, the white British, who have to learn that being British isn't what it was. Now it is a more complex thing, involving new elements. So there must be a fresh way of seeing Britain and the choices it faces: and a new way of being British after all this time. Much thought, discussion and self-examination must go into seeing the necessity for this, what this 'new way of being British' involves and how difficult it might be to attain.

The failure to grasp this opportunity for a revitalized and broader self-definition in the face of a real failure to be human, will be more insularity, schism, bitterness and catastrophe.

The two countries, Britain and Pakistan, have been part of each other for years, usually to the advantage of Britain. They cannot now be wrenched apart, even if that were desirable. Their futures will be intermixed. What that intermix means, its moral quality, whether it is violently resisted by ignorant whites and characterized by inequality and injustice, or understood, accepted and humanized, is for all of us to decide.

This decision is not one about a small group of irrelevant people who can be contemptuously described as 'minorities'. It is about the direction of British society. About its values and how humane it can be when experiencing real difficulty and possible breakdown. It is about the respect it accords individuals, the power it gives to groups, and what it really means when it describes itself as 'democratic'. The future is in our hands.

Eight Arms to Hold You

One day at school – an all-boys comprehensive on the border between London and Kent – our music teacher told us that John Lennon and Paul McCartney didn't actually write those famous Beatles songs we loved so much.

It was 1968 and I was thirteen. For the first time in music appreciation class we were to listen to the Beatles – 'She's Leaving Home', with the bass turned off. The previous week, after some Brahms, we'd been allowed to hear a Frank Zappa record, again bassless. For Mr Hogg, our music and religious instruction teacher, the bass guitar 'obscured' the music. But hearing anything by the Beatles at school was uplifting, an act so unusually liberal it was confusing.

Mr Hogg prised open the lid of the school 'stereophonic equipment', which was kept in a big, dark wooden box and wheeled around the premises by the much-abused war-wounded caretaker. Hogg put on 'She's Leaving Home' without introduction, but as soon as it began he started his Beatles analysis.

What he said was devastating, though it was put simply, as if he were stating the obvious. These were the facts: Lennon and McCartney could not possibly have written the songs ascribed to them; it was a con – we should not be taken in by the 'Beatles', they were only front-men.

Those of us who weren't irritated by his prattling through the tune were giggling. Certainly, for a change, most of us were listening to teacher. I was perplexed. Why would anyone want to think anything so ludicrous? What was really behind this idea?

'Who did write the Beatles' songs, then, sir?' someone asked bravely. And Paul McCartney sang:

> We struggled hard all our lives to get by,
> She's leaving home after living alone,
> For so many years.

Mr Hogg told us that Brian Epstein and George Martin wrote the Lennon/McCartney songs. The Fabs only played on the records – if they did anything at all. (Hogg doubted whether their hands had actually touched the instruments.) 'Real musicians were playing on those records,' he said. Then he put the record back in its famous sleeve and changed the subject.

But I worried about Hogg's theory for days; on several occasions I was tempted to buttonhole him in the corridor and discuss it further. The more I dwelt on it alone, the more it revealed. The Mopheads couldn't even read music – how could they be geniuses?

It was unbearable to Mr Hogg that four young men without significant education could be the bearers of such talent and critical acclaim. But then Hogg had a somewhat holy attitude to culture. 'He's cultured,' he'd say of someone, the antonym of 'He's common.' Culture, even popular culture – folk-singing, for instance – was something you put on a special face for, after years of wearisome study. Culture involved a particular twitching of the nose, a faraway look (into the sublime), and a fruity pursing of the lips. Hogg knew. There was, too, a sartorial vocabulary of knowingness, with leather patches sewn on to the elbows of shiny, rancid jackets.

Obviously this was not something the Beatles had been born into. Nor had they acquired it in any recognized academy or university. No, in their early twenties, the Fabs made culture again and again, seemingly without effort, even as they mugged and winked at the cameras like schoolboys.

Sitting in my bedroom listening to the Beatles on a Grundig reel-to-reel tape-recorder, I began to see that to admit to the Beatles' genius would devastate Hogg. It would take too much else away with it. The songs that were so perfect and about recognizable common feelings – 'She Loves You', 'Please, Please Me', 'I Wanna Hold Your Hand' – were all written by Brian Epstein and George Martin because the Beatles were only boys like us: ignorant, bad-mannered and rude; boys who'd never, in a just world, do anything interesting with their lives. This implicit belief, or form of contempt, was not abstract. We felt and sometimes recognised – and Hogg's attitude towards the Beatles exemplified this – that our teachers had no respect for us as people capable of learning, of finding the world compelling and wanting to know it.

The Beatles would also be difficult for Hogg to swallow because for him there was a hierarchy among the arts. At the top were stationed classical music and poetry, beside the literary novel and great painting. In the middle would be not-so-good examples of these forms. At the bottom of the list, and scarcely considered art forms at all, were films ('the pictures'), television and, finally, the most derided – pop music.

But in that post-modern dawn – the late 1960s – I like to think that Hogg was starting to experience cultural vertigo – which was why he worried about the Beatles in the first place. He thought he knew what culture was, what counted in history, what had weight, and what you needed to know to be educated. These things were not relative, not a question of taste or decision. Notions of objectivity did exist; there were criteria and Hogg knew what the criteria were. Or at least he thought he did. But that particular form of certainty, of intellectual authority, along with many other forms of authority, was shifting. People didn't know where they were any more.

Not that you could ignore the Beatles even if you wanted to. Those rockers in suits were unique in English popular music, bigger than anyone had been before. What a pleasure it was to swing past Buckingham Palace in the bus knowing the Queen was indoors, in her slippers, watching her favourite film, *Yellow Submarine*, and humming along to 'Eleanor Rigby'. ('All the lonely people . . .')

The Beatles couldn't be as easily dismissed as the Rolling Stones, who often seemed like an ersatz American group, especially when Mick Jagger started to sing with an American accent. But the Beatles' music was supernaturally beautiful and it was English music. In it you could hear cheeky music-hall songs and send-ups, pub ballads and, more importantly, hymns. The Fabs had the voices and looks of choirboys, and their talent was so broad they could do anything – love songs, comic songs, kids' songs and sing-alongs for football crowds (at White Hart Lane, Tottenham Hotspurs' ground, we sang: 'Here, there and every-fucking-where, Jimmy Greaves, Jimmy Greaves'). They could do rock 'n' roll too, though they tended to parody it, having mastered it early on.

*

One lunch-time in the school library, not long after the incident with Hogg, I came across a copy of *Life* magazine which included hefty extracts from Hunter Davies's biography of the Beatles, the first major book about them and their childhood. It was soon stolen from the library and passed around the school, a contemporary 'Lives of the Saints'. (On the curriculum we were required to read Gerald Durrell and C. S. Forester, but we had our own books, which we discussed, just as we exchanged and discussed records. We liked *Candy, Lord of the Flies*, James Bond, Mervyn Peake, and *Sex Manners for Men*, among other things.)

Finally my parents bought the biography for my birthday. It was the first hardback I possessed and, pretending to be sick, I took the day off school to read it, with long breaks between chapters to prolong the pleasure. But *The Beatles* didn't satisfy me as I'd imagined it would. It wasn't like listening to *Revolver*, for instance, after which you felt satisfied and uplifted. The book disturbed and intoxicated me; it made me feel restless and dissatisfied with my life. After reading about the Beatles' achievements I began to think I didn't expect enough of myself, that none of us at school did really. In two years we'd start work; soon after that we'd get married and buy a small house nearby. The form of life was decided before it was properly begun.

To my surprise it turned out that the Fabs were lower-middle-class provincial boys; neither rich nor poor, their music didn't come out of hardship and nor were they culturally privileged. Lennon was rough, but it wasn't poverty that made him hard-edged. The Liverpool Institute, attended by Paul and George, was a good grammar school. McCartney's father had been well enough off for Paul and his brother Michael to have piano lessons. Later, his father bought him a guitar.

We had no life guides or role models among politicians, military types or religious figures, or even film stars for that matter, as our parents did. Footballers and pop stars were the revered figures of my generation and the Beatles, more than anyone, were exemplary for countless young people. If coming from the wrong class restricts your sense of what you can be, then none of us thought we'd become doctors, lawyers, scientists, politicians.

We were scheduled to be clerks, civil servants, insurance managers and travel agents.

Not that leading some kind of creative life was entirely impossible. In the mid-1960s the media was starting to grow. There was a demand for designers, graphic artists and the like. In our art lessons we designed toothpaste boxes and record sleeves to prepare for the possibility of going to art school. Now, these were very highly regarded among the kids; they were known to be anarchic places, the sources of British pop art, numerous pop groups and the generators of such luminaries as Pete Townshend, Keith Richards, Ray Davies and John Lennon. Along with the Royal Court and the drama corridor of the BBC, the art schools were the most important post-war British cultural institution, and some lucky kids escaped into them. Once, I ran away from school to spend the day at the local art college. In the corridors where they sat cross-legged on the floor, the kids had dishevelled hair and paint-splattered clothes. A band was rehearsing in the dining hall. They liked being there so much they stayed till midnight. Round the back entrance there were condoms in the grass.

But these kids were destined to be commercial artists, which was, at least, 'proper work'. Commercial art was OK but anything that veered too closely towards pure art caused embarrassment; it was pretentious. Even education fell into this trap. When, later, I went to college, our neighbours would turn in their furry slippers and housecoats to stare and tut-tut to each other as I walked down the street in my Army-surplus greatcoat, carrying a pile of library books. I like to think it was the books rather than the coat they were objecting to – the idea that they were financing my uselessness through their taxes. Surely nurturing my brain could be of no possible benefit to the world; it would only render me more argumentative – create an intelligentsia and you're only producing criticism for the future.

(For some reason I've been long under the impression that this hatred for education is a specifically English tendency. I've never imagined the Scots, Irish or Welsh, and certainly no immigrant group, hating the idea of elevation through the mind in quite the same way. Anyhow, it would be a couple of decades before the combined neighbours of south-east England could take their revenge on education via their collective embodiment – Thatcher.)

I could, then, at least have been training to be an apprentice. But, unfortunately for the neighbours, we had seen *A Hard Day's Night* at Bromley Odeon. Along with our mothers, we screamed all through it, fingers stuck in our ears. And afterwards we didn't know what to do with ourselves, where to go, how to exorcize this passion the Beatles had stoked up. The ordinary wasn't enough; we couldn't accept only the everyday now! We desired ecstasy, the extraordinary, magnificence – today!

For most, this pleasure lasted only a few hours and then faded. But for others it opened a door to the sort of life that might, one day, be lived. And so the Beatles came to represent opportunity and possibility. They were careers officers, a myth for us to live by, a light for us to follow.

How could this be? How was it that of all the groups to emerge from that great pop period the Beatles were the most dangerous, the most threatening, the most subversive? Until they met Dylan and, later, dropped acid, the Beatles wore matching suits and wrote harmless love songs offering little ambiguity and no call to rebellion. They lacked Elvis's sexuality, Dylan's introspection and Jagger's surly danger. And yet . . . and yet – this is the thing – everything about the Beatles represented pleasure, and for the provincial and suburban young pleasure was only the outcome and justification of work. Pleasure was work's reward and it occurred only at weekends and after work.

But when you looked at *A Hard Day's Night* or *Help!*, it was clear that those four boys were having the time of their life: the films radiated freedom and good times. In them there was no sign of the long, slow accumulation of security and status, the year-after-year movement towards satisfaction, that we were expected to ask of life. Without conscience, duty or concern for the future, everything about the Beatles spoke of enjoyment, abandon and attention to the needs of the self. The Beatles became heroes to the young because they were not deferential: no authority had broken their spirit; they were confident and funny; they answered back; no one put them down. It was this independence, creativity and earning-power that worried Hogg about the Beatles. Their naïve hedonism and dazzling accomplishments were too paradoxical. For Hogg to wholeheartedly approve of them was like saying crime paid. But to dismiss the new world of the 1960s was to admit to being old and out of touch.

There was one final strategy that the defenders of the straight world developed at this time. It was a common stand-by of the neighbours. They argued that the talent of such groups was shallow. The easy money would soon be spent, squandered on objects the groups would be too jejune to appreciate. These musicians couldn't think about the future. What fools they were to forfeit the possibility of a secure job for the pleasure of having teenagers worship them for six months.

This sneering 'anyone-can-do-it' attitude to the Beatles wasn't necessarily a bad thing. Anyone could have a group – and they did. But it was obvious from early on that the Beatles were not a two-hit group like the Merseybeats or Freddie and the Dreamers. And around the time that Hogg was worrying about the authorship of 'I Saw Her Standing There' and turning down the bass on 'She's Leaving Home', just as he was getting himself used to them, the Beatles were doing something that had never been done before. They were writing songs about drugs, songs that could be fully comprehended only by people who took drugs, songs designed to be enjoyed all the more if you were stoned when you listened to them.

And Paul McCartney had admitted to using drugs, specifically LSD. This news was very shocking then. For me, the only association that drugs conjured up was of skinny Chinese junkies in squalid opium dens and morphine addicts in B movies; there had also been the wife in *Long Day's Journey into Night*. What were the Mopheads doing to themselves? Where were they taking us?

On Peter Blake's cover for *Sgt Pepper*, between Sir Robert Peel and Terry Southern, is an ex-Etonian novelist mentioned in *Remembrance of Things Past* and considered by Proust to be a genius – Aldous Huxley. Huxley first took mescalin in 1953, twelve years before the Beatles used LSD. He took psychedelic drugs eleven times, including on his death bed, when his wife injected him with LSD. During his first trip Huxley felt himself turning into four bamboo chair legs. As the folds of his grey flannel trousers became 'charged with is-ness' the world became a compelling, unpredictable, living and breathing organism. In this transfigured universe Huxley realized both his fear of and need for the 'marvellous'; one of the soul's principal appetites was for 'transcendence'. In an alienated, routine world ruled by habit, the urge for escape, for euphoria, for heightened sensation, could not be denied.

Despite his enthusiasm for LSD, when Huxley took psilocybin with Timothy Leary at Harvard he was alarmed by Leary's ideas about the wider use of psychedelic drugs. He thought Leary was an 'ass' and felt that LSD, if it were to be widely tried at all, should be given to the cultural élite – to artists, psychologists, philosophers and writers. It was important that psychedelic drugs be used seriously, primarily as aids to contemplation. Certainly they changed nothing in the world, being 'incompatible with action and even with the will to action'. Huxley was especially nervous about the aphrodisiac qualities of LSD and wrote to Leary: 'I strongly urge you not to let the sexual cat out of the bag. We've stirred up enough trouble suggesting that drugs can stimulate aesthetic and religious experience.'

But there was nothing Huxley could do to keep the 'cat' in the bag. In 1961 Leary gave LSD to Allen Ginsberg, who became convinced the drug contained the possibilities for political change. Four years later the Beatles met Ginsberg through Bob Dylan. At his own birthday party Ginsberg was naked apart from a pair of underpants on his head and a 'do not disturb' sign tied to his penis. Later, Lennon was to learn a lot from Ginsberg's style of self-exhibition as protest, but on this occasion he shrank from Ginsberg, saying: 'You don't do that in front of the birds!'

Throughout the second half of the 1960s the Beatles functioned as that rare but necessary and important channel, popularizers of esoteric ideas – about mysticism, about different forms of political involvement and about drugs. Many of these ideas originated with Huxley. The Beatles could seduce the world partly because of their innocence. They were, basically, good boys who became bad boys. And when they became bad boys, they took a lot of people with them.

Lennon claimed to have 'tripped' hundreds of times, and he

was just the sort to become interested in unusual states of mind. LSD creates euphoria and suspends inhibition; it may make us aware of life's intense flavour. In the tripper's escalation of awareness, the memory is stimulated too. Lennon knew the source of his art was the past, and his acid songs were full of melancholy, self-examination and regret. It's no surprise that *Sgt Pepper*, which at one time was to include 'Strawberry Fields' and 'Penny Lane', was originally intended to be an album of songs about Lennon and McCartney's Liverpool childhood.

Soon the Beatles started to wear clothes designed to be read by people who were stoned. God knows how much 'is-ness' Huxley would have felt had he seen John Lennon in 1967, when he was reportedly wearing a green flower-patterned shirt, red cord trousers, yellow socks and a sporran in which he carried his loose change and keys. These weren't the cheap but hip adaptations of work clothes that young males had worn since the late 1940s – Levi jackets and jeans, sneakers, work boots or DMs, baseball caps, leather jackets – democratic styles practical for work. The Beatles had rejected this conception of work. Like Baudelairean dandies they could afford to dress ironically and effeminately, for each other, for fun, beyond the constraints of the ordinary. Stepping out into that struggling post-war world steeped in memories of recent devastation and fear – the war was closer to them than *Sgt Pepper* is to me today – wearing shimmering bandsman's outfits, crushed velvet, peach-coloured silk and long hair, their clothes were gloriously non-functional, identifying their creativity and the pleasures of drug-taking.

By 1966 the Beatles behaved as if they spoke directly to the whole world. This was not a mistake: they were at the centre of life for millions of young people in the West. And certainly they're the only mere pop group you could remove from history and suggest that culturally, without them, things would have been significantly different. All this meant that what they did was influential and important. At this time, before people were aware of the power of the media, the social changes the Beatles sanctioned had happened practically before anyone noticed. Musicians have always been involved with drugs, but the Beatles were the first to parade their particular drug-use – marijuana and LSD – publicly and without shame. They never claimed, as musicians do now – when found out – that drugs were a 'problem' for them. And unlike the Rolling Stones, they were never humiliated for drug-taking or turned into outlaws. There's a story that at a bust at Keith Richard's house in 1967, before the police went in they waited for George Harrison to leave. The Beatles made taking drugs seem an enjoyable, fashionable and liberating experience: like them, you would see and feel in ways you hadn't imagined possible. Their endorsement, far more than that of any other group or individual, removed drugs from their sub-cultural, avant-garde and generally squalid associations, making them part of mainstream youth activity. Since then, illegal drugs have accompanied music, fashion and dance as part of what it is to be young in the West.

Allen Ginsberg called the Beatles 'the paradigm of the age', and they were indeed condemned to live out their period in all its foolishness, extremity and commendable idealism. Countless preoccupations of the time were expressed through the Fabs. Even Apple Corps was a characteristic 1960s notion: an attempt to run a business venture in an informal, creative and non-materialistic way.

Whatever they did and however it went wrong, the Beatles were always on top of things musically, and perhaps it is this, paradoxically, that made their end inevitable. The loss of control that psychedelic drugs can involve, the political anger of the 1960s and its anti-authoritarian violence, the foolishness and inauthenticity of being pop stars at all, rarely violates the highly finished surface of their music. Songs like 'Revolution' and 'Helter Skelter' attempt to express unstructured or deeply felt passions, but the Beatles are too controlled to let their music fray. It never felt as though the band was going to disintegrate through sheer force of feeling, as with Hendrix, the Who or the Velvet Underground. Their ability was so extensive that all madness could be contained within a song. Even 'Strawberry Fields' and 'I Am the Walrus' are finally engineered and controlled. The exception is 'Revolution No.9', which Lennon had to fight to keep on the *White Album*; he wanted to smash through the organization and accomplished form of his pop music. But Lennon had to leave the Beatles to continue in that direction and it wasn't until his first solo album that he was able to strip away the Beatle frippery for the raw feeling he was after.

At least, Lennon wanted to do this. In the 1970s, the liberation tendencies of the 1960s bifurcated into two streams – hedonism, self-aggrandisement and decay, represented by the Stones; and serious politics and self-exploration, represented by Lennon. He continued to be actively involved in the obsessions of the time, both as initiate and leader, which is what makes him the central cultural figure of the age, as Brecht was, for instance, in the 1930s and 1940s.

But to continue to develop Lennon had to leave the containment of the Beatles and move to America. He had to break up the Beatles to lead an interesting life.

I heard a tape the other day of a John Lennon interview. What struck me, what took me back irresistibly, was realizing how much I loved his voice and how inextricably bound up it was with my own growing up. It was a voice I must have heard almost every day for years, on television, radio or record. It was more exceptional then than it is now, not being the voice of the BBC or of southern England, or of a politician; it was neither emollient nor instructing, it was direct and very hip. It pleased without trying to. Lennon's voice continues to intrigue me, and not just for nostalgic reasons, perhaps because of the range of what it says. It's a strong but cruel and harsh voice; not one you'd want to hear putting you down. It's naughty, vastly melancholic and knowing too, full of self-doubt, self-confidence and humour. It's expressive, charming and sensual; there's little concealment in it, as there is in George Harrison's voice, for example. It is aggressive and combative but the violence in it is attractive since it seems to emerge out of a passionate involvement with the world. It's the voice of someone who is alive in both feeling and mind; it comes from someone who has understood their own experience and knows their value.

The only other public voice I know that represents so much, that seems to have spoken relentlessly to me for years, bringing with it a whole view of life – though from the dark side – is that of Margaret Thatcher. When she made her 'St Francis of Assisi' speech outside 10 Downing Street after winning the 1979

General Election, I laughed aloud at the voice alone. It was impenetrable to me that anyone could have voted for a sound that was so cold, so pompous, so clearly insincere, ridiculous and generally absurd.

In this same voice, and speaking of her childhood, Thatcher once said that she felt that 'To pursue pleasure for its own sake was wrong'.

In retrospect it isn't surprising that the 1980s *mélange* of liberal economics and Thatcher's pre-war Methodist priggishness would embody a reaction to the pleasure-seeking of the 1960s and 1970s, as if people felt ashamed, guilty and angry about having gone too far, as if they'd enjoyed themselves too much. The greatest surprise was had by the Left – the ideological left rather than the pragmatic Labour Party – which believed it had, during the 1970s, made immeasurable progress since *Sgt Pepper*, penetrating the media and the Labour Party, the universities and the law, fanning out and reinforcing itself in various organizations like the gay, black and women's movements. The 1960s was a romantic period and Lennon a great romantic hero, both as poet and political icon. Few thought that what he represented would all end so quickly and easily, that the Left would simply hand over the moral advantage and their established positions in the country as if they hadn't fought for them initially.

Thatcher's trope against feeling was a resurrection of control, a repudiation of the sensual, of self-indulgence in any form, self-exploration and the messiness of non-productive creativity, often specifically targeted against the 'permissive' 1960s. Thatcher's colleague Norman Tebbit characterized this suburban view of the Beatle period with excellent vehemence, calling it: 'The insufferable, smug, sanctimonious, naïve, guilt-ridden, wet, pink orthodoxy of that sunset home of that third-rate decade, the 60s.'

The amusing thing is that Thatcher's attempt to convert Britain to an American-style business-based society has failed. It is not something that could possibly have taken in such a complacent and divided land, especially one lacking a self-help culture. Only the immigrants in Britain have it: they have much to fight for and much to gain through being entrepreneurial. But it's as if no one else can be bothered – they're too mature to fall for such ideas.

Ironically, the glory, or, let us say, the substantial achievements of Britain in its ungracious decline, has been its art. There is here a tradition of culture dissent (or argument or cussedness) caused by the disaffections and resentments endemic in a class-bound society, which fed the best fiction of the 1960s, the theatre of the 1960s and 1970s, and the cinema of the early 1980s. But principally and more prolifically, reaching a world-wide audience and being innovative and challenging, there is the production of pop music – the richest cultural form of post-war Britain. Ryszard Kapuscinski in 'Shah of Shahs' quotes a Tehran carpet salesman: 'What have we given the world? We have given poetry, the miniature, and carpets. As you can see, these are all useless things from the productive viewpoint. But it is through such things that we have expressed our true selves.'

The Beatles are the godhead of British pop, the hallmark of excellence in song-writing and, as importantly, in the interweaving of music and life. They set the agenda for what was possible in pop music after them. And Lennon, especially, in refusing to be a career pop star and dissociating himself from the politics of his time, saw, in the 1970s, pop becoming explicitly involved in social issues. In 1976 Eric Clapton interrupted a concert he was giving in Birmingham to make a speech in support of Enoch Powell. The incident led to the setting up of Rock Against Racism. Using pop music as an instrument of solidarity, as resistance and propaganda, it was an effective movement against the National Front at a time when official politics – the Labour Party – were incapable of taking direct action around immediate street issues. And punk too, of course, emerged partly out of the unemployment, enervation and directionlessness of the mid-1970s.

During the 1980s, Thatcherism discredited such disinterested and unprofitable professions as teaching, and yet failed, as I've said, to implant a forging culture of self-help. Today, as then, few British people believe that nothing will be denied them if only they work hard enough, as many Americans, for instance, appear to believe. Most British know for a fact that, whatever they do, they can't crash through the constraints of the class system and all the prejudices and instincts for exclusion that it contains. But pop music is the one area in which this belief in mobility, reward and opportunity does exist.

Fortunately the British school system can be incompetent, liberal and so lacking in self-belief that it lacks the conviction to crush the creativity of young people, which does, therefore, continue to flourish in the interstices of authority, in the school corridor and after four o'clock, as it were. The crucial thing is to have education that doesn't stamp out the desire to learn, that attempts to educate while the instincts of young people – which desire to be stimulated but in very particular things, like sport, pop music and television – flower in spite of the teacher's requirement to educate. The sort of education that Thatcherism needed as a base – hard-line, conformist, medicinal, providing soldiers for the trenches of business wars and not education for its own sake – is actually against the tone or feeling of an England that is not naturally competitive, not being desperate enough, though desperate conditions were beginning to be created.

Since Hogg first played 'She's Leaving Home', the media has expanded unimaginably, but pop music remains one area accessible to all, both for spectators and, especially, for participants. The cinema is too expensive, the novel too refined and exclusive, the theatre too poor and middle-class, and television too complicated and rigid. Music is simpler to get into. And pop musicians never have to ask themselves – in the way that writers, for instance, constantly have to – who is my audience, who am I writing for and what am I trying to say? It is art for their own sakes, and art which connects with a substantial audience hungry for a new product, an audience which is, by now, soaked in the history of pop music and is sophisticated, responsive and knowledgeable.

And so there has been in Britain since the mid-1960s a stream of fantastically accomplished music, encompassing punk and New Wave, northern soul, reggae, hip-hop, rap, acid jazz and house. The Left, in its puritanical way, has frequently dismissed pop as capitalist pap, preferring folk and other 'traditional' music. But it is pop that has spoken of ordinary experience with far more precision, real knowledge and wit than, say, British fiction of the equivalent period. And you can't dance to fiction.

In the 1980s, during Thatcher's 'permanent revolution', there was much talk of identity, race, nationality, history and, naturally, culture. But pop music, which has bound young people together more than anything else, was usually left out. But this tradition of joyous and lively music created by young people from state schools, kids from whom little was expected, has made a form of self-awareness, entertainment and effective criticism that deserves to be acknowledged and applauded but never institutionalized. But then that is up to the bands and doesn't look like happening, pop music being a rebellious form in itself if it is to be any good. And the Beatles, the most likely candidates ever for institutionalization, finally repudiated that particular death through the good sense of John Lennon, who gave back his MBE, climbed inside a white bag and wrote 'Cold Turkey'.

Bradford

Some time ago, I noticed that there was something unusual about the city of Bradford, something that distinguished it from other northern industrial cities.

To begin with, there was Ray Honeyford. Three years ago Honeyford, the headmaster of Bradford's Drummond Middle School, wrote a short, three-page article that was published in the *Salisbury Review*. The *Salisbury Review* has a circulation of about 1,000, but the impact of Honeyford's article was felt beyond the magazine's readership. It was discussed in the *Yorkshire Post* and reprinted in the local *Telegraph and Argus*. A parents' group demanded Honeyford's resignation. His school was then boycotted, and children, instructed by their parents not to attend classes, gathered outside, shouting abuse at the man who weeks before was their teacher. There were fights, sometimes physical brawls, between local leaders and politicians. The 'Honeyford Affair', as it became known, attracted so much attention that it became common every morning to come upon national journalists and television crews outside the school. And when it was finally resolved that Honeyford had to go, the Bradford district council had to pay him over £160,000 to get him to leave: ten times his annual salary.

But there were other things about Bradford. The Yorkshire Ripper was from Bradford. The prostitutes who came down to London on the train on 'cheap-day return' tickets were from Bradford. At a time when the game of soccer was threatened by so many troubles, Bradford seemed to have troubles of the most extreme kind. Days after the deaths in Brussels at the Heysel stadium, forty-seven Bradford football supporters were killed in one of the worst fires in the history of the sport. Eighteen months later, there was yet another fire, and a match stopped because of crowd violence.

There was more: there was unemployment in excess of twenty percent; there was a prominent branch of the National Front; there were regular racial attacks on taxi drivers; there were stories of forced emigration; there was a mayor from a village in

Pakistan. Bradford, I felt, was a place I had to see for myself, because it seemed that so many important issues, of race, culture, nationalism, and education, were evident in an extremely concentrated way in this medium-sized city of 400,000 people, situated between the much larger cities of Manchester and Leeds. These were issues that related to the whole notion of what it was to be British and what that would mean in the future. Bradford seemed to be a microcosm of a larger British society that was struggling to find a sense of itself, even as it was undergoing radical change. And it was a struggle not seen by the people governing the country, who, after all, had been brought up in a world far different from today's. In 1945, England ruled over six hundred million people. And there were few black faces on its streets.

The first thing you notice as you get on the Inter-City train to Bradford is that the first three carriages are first class. These are followed by the first-class restaurant car. Then you are free to sit down. But if the train is packed and you cannot find an empty seat, you have to stand. You stand for the whole journey, with other people lying on the floor around you, and you look through at the empty seats in the first-class carriages where men sit in their shirt-sleeves doing important work and not looking up. The ticket collector has to climb over us to get to them.

Like the porters on the station, the ticket collector was black, probably of West Indian origin. In other words, black British. Most of the men fixing the railway line, in their luminous orange jackets, with pickaxes over their shoulders, were also black. The guard on the train was Pakistani, or should I say another Briton, probably born here, and therefore 'black'.

When I got to Bradford I took a taxi. It was simple: Bradford is full of taxis. Raise an arm and three taxis rush at you. Like most taxi drivers in Bradford, the driver was Asian and his car had furry, bright purple seats, covered with the kind of material people in the suburbs sometimes put on the lids of their toilets. It smelled of perfume, and Indian music was playing. The taxi driver had a Bradford-Pakistani accent, a cross between the north of England and Lahore, which sounds odd the first few times you hear it. Mentioning the accent irritates people in

Bradford. How else do you expect people to talk? they say. And they are right. But hearing it for the first time disconcerted me because I found that I associated northern accents with white faces, with people who eat puddings, with Geoffrey Boycott and Roy Hattersley.

We drove up a steep hill, which overlooked the city. In the distance there were modern buildings and among them the older mill chimneys and factories with boarded-up windows. We passed Priestley Road. J. B. Priestley was born in Bradford, and in the early sixties both John Braine and Alan Sillitoe set novels here. I wondered what the writing of the next fifteen years would be like. There were, I was to learn, stories in abundance to be told.

The previous day I had watched one of my favourite films, Keith Waterhouse and Willis Hall's *Billy Liar*, also written in the early sixties. Billy works for an undertaker and there is a scene in which Billy tries to seduce one of his old girlfriends in a graveyard. Now I passed that old graveyard. It was full of monstrous mausoleums, some with spires thirty feet high; others were works of architecture in themselves, with arches, urns and roofs. They dated from the late nineteenth century and contained the bones of the great mill barons and their families. In *The Waste Land* T. S. Eliot wrote of the 'silk hat on a Bradford millionaire'. Now the mills and the millionaires had nearly disappeared. In the cemetery there were some white youths on a Youth Opportunity Scheme, hacking unenthusiastically at the weeds, clearing a path. This was the only work that could be found for them, doing up the cemetery.

I was staying in a house near the cemetery. The houses were of a good size, well-built with three bedrooms and lofts. Their front doors were open and the street was full of kids running in and out. Women constantly crossed the street and stood on each others' doorsteps, talking. An old man with a stick walked along slowly. He stopped to pat a child who was crying so much I thought she would explode. He carried on patting her head, and she carried on crying, until finally he decided to enter the house and fetched the child's young sister.

The houses were overcrowded – if you looked inside you would usually see five or six adults sitting in the front room – and there wasn't much furniture: often the linoleum on the floor was torn and curling, and a bare lightbulb hung from the ceiling. The wallpaper was peeling from the walls.

Each house had a concrete yard at the back, where women and young female children were always hanging out the washing: the cleaning of clothes appeared never to stop. There was one man – his house was especially run-down – who had recently acquired a new car. He walked round and round it; he was proud of his car, and occasionally caressed it.

It was everything I imagined a Bradford working-class community would be like, except that there was one difference. Everyone I'd seen since I arrived was Pakistani. I had yet to see a white face.

The women covered their heads. And while the older ones wore jumpers and overcoats, underneath they, like the young girls, wore *salwar kamiz*, the Pakistani long tops over baggy trousers. If I ignored the dark Victorian buildings around me, I could imagine that everyone was back in their village in Pakistan.

That evening, Jane – the friend I was staying with – and I decided to go out. We walked back down the hill and into the centre of town. It looked like many other town centres in Britain. The subways under the roundabouts stank of urine; graffiti defaced them and lakes of rain-water gathered at the bottom of the stairs. There was a massive shopping centre with unnatural lighting; some kids were rollerskating through it, pursued by three pink-faced security guards in paramilitary outfits. the shops were also the same: Rymans, Smiths, Dixons, the National Westminster Bank. I hadn't become accustomed to Bradford and found myself making simple comparisons with London. The clothes people wore were shabby and old; they looked as if they'd been bought in jumble sales or second-hand shops. And their faces had an unhealthy aspect: some were malnourished.

As we crossed the city, I could see that some parts looked old-fashioned. They reminded me of my English grandfather and the Britain of my childhood: pigeon-keeping, greyhound racing, roast beef eating and pianos in pubs. Outside the centre, there were shops you'd rarely see in London now: drapers, iron-mongers, fish and chip shops that still used newspaper wrappers, barber's shops with photographs in the window of men with Everly Brothers haircuts. And here, among all this, I also saw the Islamic Library and the Ambala Sweet Centre where you could buy spices: dhaniya, haldi, garam masala, and dhal and ladies' fingers. There were Asian video shops where you could buy tapes of the songs of Master Sajjad, Nayyara, Alamgir, Nazeen and M. Ali Shahaiky.

Jane and I went to a bar. It was a cross between a pub and a night-club. At the entrance the bouncer laid his hands on my shoulders and told me I could not go in.

'Why not?' I asked.

'You're not wearing any trousers.'

I looked down at my legs in astonishment.

'Are you sure?' I asked.

'No trousers,' he said, 'no entry.'

Jeans, it seems, were not acceptable.

We walked on to another place. This time we got in. It too was very smart and entirely white. The young men had dressed up in open-necked shirts, Top Shop grey slacks and Ravel loafers. They stood around quietly in groups. The young women had also gone to a lot of trouble: some of them looked like models, in their extravagant dresses and high heels. But the women and the men were not talking to each other. We had a drink and left. Jane said she wanted me to see a working men's club.

The working men's club turned out to be near an estate, populated, like most Bradford estates, mostly by whites. The Asians tended to own their homes. They had difficulty acquiring council houses or flats, and were harassed and abused when they moved on to white estates.

The estate was scruffy: some of the flats were boarded up, rubbish blew about; the balconies looked as if they were about to crash off the side of the building. The club itself was in a large modern building. We weren't members of course, but the man on the door agreed to let us in.

There were three large rooms. One was like a pub; another was a snooker room. In the largest room at least 150 people sat around tables in families. At one end was a stage. A white man in evening dress was banging furiously at a drum-kit. Another played the organ. The noise was unbearable.

At the bar, it was mostly elderly men. They sat beside each other. But they didn't talk. They had drawn, pale faces and thin, narrow bodies that expanded dramatically at the stomach and then disappeared into the massive jutting band of their trousers. They had little legs. They wore suits, the men. They had dressed up for the evening.

Here there were no Asians either, and I wanted to go to an Asian bar, but it was getting late and the bars were closing, at ten-thirty as they do outside London. We got a taxi and drove across town. The streets got rougher and rougher. We left the main road and suddenly were in a leafy, almost suburban area. The houses here were large, occupied I imagined by clerks, insurance salesmen, business people. We stopped outside a detached three-storey house that seemed to be surrounded by an extraordinary amount of darkness and shadow. There was one light on, in the kitchen, and the woman inside was Sonia Sutcliffe, the wife of the Yorkshire Ripper, an ex-schoolteacher. I thought of Peter Sutcliffe telling his wife he was the Yorkshire Ripper. He had wanted to tell her himself; he insisted on it. Many of his victims had come from the surrounding area.

The surrounding area was mostly an Asian district and here the pubs stayed open late, sometimes until two in the morning. There were no trouser rules.

During the day in this part of town the Asian kids would be playing in the streets. The women, most of them uneducated, illiterate, unable to speak English, would talk in doorways as they did where I was staying.

It was around midnight, and men were only now leaving their houses – the women remaining behind with the children – and walking down the street to the pub. Jane said it stayed open late with police permission. It gave the police an opportunity to find out what was going on: their spies and informers could keep an eye on people. Wherever you went in Bradford, people talked about spies and informers: who was and who wasn't. I'd never known anything like it, but then I'd never known any other city, except perhaps Karachi, in which politics was such a dominant part of daily life. Apparently there was money to be made working for the police and reporting what was going on: what the Asian militants were doing; what the racists were doing; who the journalists were talking to; what attacks or demonstrations were planned; what vigilante groups were being formed.

The pub was packed with Asian men and they still kept arriving. They knew each other and embraced enthusiastically. There were few women and all but three were white. Asian men and white women kissed in corners. As we squeezed in, Jane said she knew several white women who were having affairs with Asian men, affairs that had sometimes gone on for years. The men had married Pakistani women, often out of family pressure, and frequently the women were from the villages. The Asian women had a terrible time in Bradford.

The music was loud and some people were dancing, elbow to elbow, only able in the crush to shake their heads and shuffle their feet. There was a lot of very un-Islamic drinking. I noticed two Asian girls. They stood out, with their bright jewellery and pretty clothes. They were with Asian men. Their men looked inhibited and the girls left early. Jane, who was a journalist, recognized a number of prostitutes in the pub. She'd interviewed them at the time of the Ripper. One stood by Jane and kept pulling at her jumper. 'Where did you get that jumper? How much was it?' she kept saying. Jane said the prostitutes hadn't stopped work during the time of the Ripper. They couldn't afford to. Instead, they'd worked in pairs, one girl fucking the man, while the other stood by with a knife in her hand.

In 1993, when J. B. Priestley was preparing his *English Journey*, he found three Englands. There was guide-book England, of palaces and forests; nineteenth-century industrial England of factories and suburbs; and contemporary England of by-passes and suburbs. Now, half a century later, there is another England as well: the inner city.

In front of me, in this pub, there were five or six gay men and two lesbian couples. Three white kids wore black leather jackets and had mohicans: their mauve, red and yellow hair stood up straight for a good twelve inches and curved across their heads like a feather glued on its thin edge to a billiard ball. And there were the Asians. This was not one large solid community with a shared outlook, common beliefs and an established form of life; not Orwell's 'one family with the wrong members in control'. It was diverse, disparate, strikingly various.

Jane introduced me to a young Asian man, an activist and local political star from his time of being on trial as one of the Bradford Twelve. I was pleased to meet him. In 1981, a group of twelve youths, fearing a racial attack in the aftermath of the terrible assault on Asians by skinheads in Southall in London, had made a number of petrol bombs. But they were caught and charged under the Explosives Act with conspiracy – a charge normally intended for urban terrorists. It was eleven months before they were acquitted.

I greeted him enthusiastically. He, with less enthusiasm, asked me if I'd written a film called *My Beautiful Laundrette*. I said yes, I had, and he started to curse me: I was a fascist, a reactionary. He was shouting. Then he seemed to run out of words and pulled back to hit me. But just as he raised his fist, his companions grabbed his arm and dragged him away.

I said to Jane that I thought the next day we should so something less exhausting. We could visit a school.

I had heard that there was to be a ceremony for a new school that was opening, the Zakariya Girls School. The large community hall was already packed with three hundred Asian men when I arrived. Then someone took my arm, to eject me, I thought. But instead I was led to the front row, where I found myself sitting next to three white policemen and assorted white dignitaries, both women and men, in smart Sunday-school clothes.

On the high stage sat local councillors, a white Muslim in white turban and robes, and various Asian men. A white man was addressing the audience, the MP for Scarborough, Sir Michael Shaw. 'You have come into our community,' he was saying, 'and you must become part of that community. All branches must lead to one trunk, which is the British way of life. We mustn't retire to our own communities and shut ourselves out. Yet you have felt you needed schools of your own . . .'

The MP was followed by a man who appeared to be a home-grown Batley citizen. 'As a practising Roman Catholic, I sympathize with you, having had a Catholic education myself,' he said, and went on to say how good he thought the Islamic school would be.

Finally the man from the local mosque read some verses from

the Koran. The local policemen cupped their hands and lowered their heads in true multi-cultural fashion. The other whites near me, frantically looking around at each other, quickly followed suit. Then Indian sweets were brought round, which the polite English ladies picked politely at.

I left the hall and walked up the hill towards the school. The policeman followed me, holding the hands of the six or seven Asian children that surrounded him.

Batley is outside Bradford, on the way to Leeds. It is a small town surrounded by countryside and hills. The view from the hill into the valley and then up into the hills was exquisite. In the town there was a large Asian community. The Zakariya Girls School had actually been started two years ago as a 'pirate' school, not having received approval from the Department of Education until an extension was built. Now it was finished. And today it became the first high school of its kind – an Islamic school for girls – to be officially registered under the Education Act. As a pirate school it had been a large, overcrowded old house on the top of a hill. Now, outside, was a new two-storey building. It was spacious, clean, modern.

I went in and looked around. Most of the books were on the Koran or Islam, on prayer or on the prophet Mohammed. The walls were covered with verses from the Koran. And despite its being a girls' school there were no girls there and no Asian women, just the men and lots of little boys in green, blue and brown caps, running about.

The idea for the school had been the pop star Cat Stevens's, and he had raised most of the money for it privately, it was said, from Saudi Arabia. Stevens, who had changed his name to Yusaf Islam, was quoted as saying that he had tried everything, running the gamut of international novelties to find spiritual satisfaction: materialism, sex, drugs, Buddhism, Christianity and finally Islam. I wondered if it was entirely arbitrary that he'd ended with Islam or whether perhaps today, the circumstances being slightly different, we could as easily have been at the opening of a Buddhist school.

Yusaf Islam was not at the school but his assistant, Ibrahim, was. Ibrahim was the white Muslim in the white robes with the white turban who spoke earlier. There was supposed to be a press conference, but nothing was happening; everything was disorganized. Ibrahim came and sat beside me. I asked him if he'd talk about the school. He was, he said, very keen; the school had been the result of so much effort and organization, so much goodness. I looked at him. He seemed preternaturally good and calm.

Ibrahim was from Newcastle, and had a long ginger beard. (I remembered someone saying to me in Pakistan that the only growth industry in Islamic countries was in human hair on the face.) Ibrahim's epiphany had occurred on a trip to South Africa. There, seeing black and white men praying together in a mosque, he decided to convert to Islam.

He told me about the way the school worked. The human face, for instance, or the face of any animate being, could not be represented at the school. And dancing would not be encouraged, nor the playing of musical instruments. Surely, he said, looking at me, his face full of conviction, the human voice was expressive enough? When I said this would probably rule out the possibility of the girls taking either art or music O-Levels, he nodded sadly and admitted that it would.

And modern literature? I asked.

He nodded sadly again and said it would be studied 'in a critical light'.

I said I was glad to hear it. But what about science?

That was to be studied in a critical light too, since – and here he took a deep breath – he didn't accept Darwinism or any theory of evolution because, well, because the presence of monkeys who hadn't changed into men disproved it all.

I took another close look at him. He obviously believed these things. But why was he being so apologetic?

As I walked back down the hill I thought about the issues raised by the Zakariya Girls School. There were times, I thought, when to be accommodating you had to bend over backwards so far that you fell over. Since the mid-sixties the English liberal has seen the traditional hierarchies and divisions of British life challenged, if not destroyed. Assumptions of irrevocable, useful and moral differences – between classes, men and women, gays and straights, older and younger people, developed and underdeveloped societies – had changed for good. The commonly made distinction between 'higher' and 'lower' cultures had become suspect. It had become questionable philosophically to apply criteria of judgement available in one society to events in another: there could not be any independent or bridging method of evaluation. And it followed that we should be able, as a broad, humane and pluralistic society, to sustain a wide range of disparate groups living in their own way. And if one of these groups wanted *halal* meat, Islamic schools, anti-Darwinism and an intimate knowledge of the Koran for its girls, so be it. As it was, there had been Catholic schools and Jewish schools for years.

But Islamic schools like the one in Batley appeared to violate the principles of a liberal education, and the very ideas to which the school owed its existence. And because of the community's religious beliefs, so important to its members, the future prospects for the girls were reduced. Was that the choice they had made? Did the Asian community really want this kind of separate education anyway? And if it did, how many wanted it? Or was it only a few earnest and repressed believers, all men, frightened of England and their daughters' sexuality?

The house Delius was born in, in Bradford, was now the Council of Mosques, which looked after the interests of the Bradford Muslims. There are 60,000 Muslims and thirty Muslim organizations in Bradford. Chowdhury Khan, the President of the Council, told me about the relations between men and women in Islam and the problem of girls' schools.

He said there were no women in the Council because 'we respect them too much.' I mentioned that I found this a little perplexing, but he ignored me, adding that this is also why women were not encouraged to have jobs or careers.

'Women's interests,' he said confidently, 'are being looked after.'

And the girls'?

After the age of twelve, he said, women should not mix with men. That was why more single-sex schools were required in Bradford. The local council had agreed that this was desirable and would provide more single-sex schools when resources were available. He added that despite the Labour Manifesto, Neil Kinnock approved of this.

I said I doubted this.

Anyway, he continued, the local Labour Party was lobbying for more single-sex schools after having tried, in the sixties, to provide mixed-sex schools. But – and this he emphasized – the Council of Mosques wanted single-sex schools *not* Islamic ones or racially segregated schools. He banged on his desk, No, no, no! No apartheid!

He wanted the state to understand that, while Muslim children would inevitably become westernized – they were reconciled to that – they still wanted their children to learn about Islam at school, to learn subcontinental languages and be taught the history, politics and geography of India, Pakistan and Bangladesh. Surely, he added, the white British would be interested in this too. After all, the relations between England and the subcontinent had always been closer than those between Britain and France, say.

I found Chowdhury Khan to be a difficult and sometimes strange man. But his values, and the values of the Council he represented, are fairly straightforward. He believes in the pre-eminent value of the family and, for example, the importance of religion in establishing morality. He also believes in the innately inferior position of women. He dislikes liberalism in all its forms, and is an advocate of severe and vengeful retribution against law-breakers.

These are extremely conservative and traditional views. But they are also, isolated from the specifics of their subcontinental context, the values championed by Ray Honeyford, among others. There were a number of interesting ironies developing.

I sought out the younger, more militant section of the community. How did its members see their places in Britain?

When I was in my teens, in the mid-sixties, there was much talk of the 'problems' that kids of my colour and generation faced in Britain because of our racial mix or because our parents were immigrants. We didn't know where we belonged, it was said; we were neither fish nor fowl. I remember reading that kind of thing in the newspaper. We were frequently referred to as 'second-generation immigrants' just so there was no mistake about our not really belonging in Britain. We were 'Britain's children without a home'. The phrase 'caught between two cultures' was a favourite. It was a little too triumphant for me. Anyway, this view was wrong. It has been easier for us than for our parents. For them Britain really had been a strange land and it must have been hard to feel part of a society if you had spent a good deal of your life elsewhere and intended to return: most immigrants from the Indian subcontinent came to Britain to make money and then go home. Most of the Pakistanis in Bradford had come from one specific district, Mirpur, because that was where the Bradford mill-owners happened to look for cheap labour twenty-five years ago. And many, once here, stayed for good; it was not possible to go back. Yet when they got older the immigrants found they hadn't really made a place for themselves in Britain. They missed the old country. They'd always thought of Britain as a kind of long stopover rather than the final resting place it would turn out to be.

But for me and the others of my generation born here, Britain was always where we belonged, even when we were told – often in terms of racial abuse – that this was not so. Far from being a conflict of cultures, our lives seemed to synthesize disparate elements: the pub, the mosque, two or three languages, rock 'n' roll, Indian films. Our extended family and our British individuality co-mingled.

Tariq was twenty-two. His office was bare in the modern style: there was a desk; there was a computer. The building was paid for by the EEC and Bradford Council. His job was to advise on the setting-up of businesses and on related legal matters. He also advised the Labour Party on its economic policy. In fact, although so young, Tariq had been active in politics for a number of years: at the age of sixteen, he had been chairman of the Asian Youth Movement, which was founded in 1978 after the National Front began marching on Bradford. But few of the other young men I'd met in Bradford had Tariq's sense of direction or ambition, including the young activists known as the Bradford Twelve. Five years after their acquittal, most of them were, like Tariq, very active – fighting deportations, monitoring racist organizations, advising on multi-cultural education – but, like other young people in Bradford, they were unemployed. They hung around the pubs; their politics were obscure; they were 'anti-fascist' but it was difficult to know what they were for. Unlike their parents, who'd come here for a specific purpose, to make a life in the affluent west away from poverty and lack of opportunity, they, born here, had inherited only pointlessness and emptiness. The emptiness, that is, derived not from racial concerns but economic ones.

Tariq took me to a Pakistani café. Bradford was full of them. They were like English working men's cafés, except the food was Pakistani, you ate with your fingers and there was always water on the table. The waiter spoke to us in Punjabi and Tariq replied. Then the waiter looked at me and asked a question. I looked vague, nodded stupidly and felt ashamed. Tariq realized I could only speak English.

How many languages did he speak?

Four: English, Malay, Urdu and Punjabi.

I told him about the school I'd visited.

Tariq was against Islamic schools. He thought they made it harder for Asian kids in Britain to get qualifications than in ordinary, mixed-race, mixed-sex schools. He said the people who wanted such schools were not representative; they just made a lot of noise and made the community look like it was made up of separatists, which it was not.

He wasn't a separatist, he said. He wanted the integration of all into the society. But for him the problem of integration was adjacent to the problem of being poor in Britain: how could people feel themselves to be active participants in the life of a society when they were suffering all the wretchedness of bad housing, poor insulation and the indignity of having their gas and electricity disconnected; or when they were turning to loan sharks to pay their bills; or when they felt themselves being dissipated by unemployment; and when they weren't being properly educated, because the resources for a proper education didn't exist.

There was one Asian in Bradford it was crucial to talk to. He'd had political power. For a year he'd been mayor, and as Britain's first Asian or black mayor he received much attention. He'd also had a terrible time.

I talked to Mohammed Ajeeb in the nineteenth-century town hall. The town hall was a monument to Bradford's long-gone splendour and pride. Later I ran into him at Bradford's superb Museum of Film, Television and Photography, where a huge photo of him and his wife was unveiled. Ajeeb is a tall, modest man, sincere, sometimes openly uncertain and highly regarded for his tenacity by the Labour leader Neil Kinnock. Ajeeb is careful in his conversation. He lacks the confident politician's polish: from him, I heard no well-articulated banalities. He is from a small village in the Punjab. When we met at the Museum, we talked about the differences between us, and he admitted that it had been quite a feat for someone like him to have got so far in Britain. In Pakistan, with its petrified feudal system, he would never have been able to transcend his background.

During his time in office, a stand at the Valley Parade football ground had burned down, killing fifty-six people and injuring 300 others. There was the Honeyford affair, about which he had been notoriously outspoken ('I cannot see,' he said in a speech that contributed to Honeyford's removal, 'the unity of our great city being destroyed by one man'). As mayor, Ajeeb moved through areas of Bradford society to which he never had access before, and the racism he experienced, both explicit and covert, was of a viciousness he hadn't anticipated. And it was relentless. His house was attacked, and he, as mayor, was forced to move; and at Grimsby Town football ground, when he presented a cheque to the families of those killed in the fire, the crowd abused him with racist slogans; finally, several thousand football supporters started chanting Honeyford's name so loudly that Ajeeb was unable to complete his speech. He received sackfuls of hate mail and few letters of support.

Ajeeb said that no culture could remain static, neither British nor Pakistani. And while groups liked to cling to the old ways and there would be conflict, eventually different groups would intermingle. For him the important thing was that minorities secure political power for themselves. At the same time, he said that, although he wanted to become a Parliamentary candidate, no one would offer him a constituency where he could stand.

This was, he thought, because he was Asian and the Labour Party feared that the white working class wouldn't vote for him. He could stand as Parliamentary candidate only in a black area, which seemed fine to him for the time being; he was prepared to do that.

There were others who weren't prepared to put up with the racism in the trade union movement and in the Labour Party itself in the way Ajeeb had. I met a middle-aged Indian man, a tax inspector, who had been in the Labour Party for at least ten years. He had offered to help canvass during the local council elections – on a white council estate. He was told that it wouldn't be to the party's advantage for him to help in a white area. He was so offended that he offered his services to the Tories. Although he hated Margaret Thatcher, he found the Tories welcomed him. He started to lecture on the subject of Asians in Britain to various Tory groups and Rotary Club dinners, until he found himself talking at the Wakefield Police College. At the Wakefield Police College he encountered the worst racists he had ever seen in his life.

He did not need to go into details. Only a few months before, at an anti-apartheid demonstration outside South Africa House in London, I'd been standing by a police line when a policeman started to talk to me. He spoke in a low voice, as if he were telling me about the traffic in Piccadilly. 'You bastards,' he said. 'We hate you, we don't want you here. Everything would be all right, there'd be none of this, if you pissed off home.' And he went on like that, fixing me with a stare. 'You wogs, you coons, you blacks, we hate you all.'

Ajeeb said that if there was anything he clung to when things became unbearable, it was the knowledge that the British electorate always rejected the far Right. They had never voted in significant numbers for neo-fascist groups like the National Front and the British National Party. Even the so-called New Right, a prominent and noisy group of journalists, lecturers and intellectuals, had no great popular following. People knew what viciousness underlay their ideas, he said.

Some of the views of the New Right, Ajeeb believed, had much in common with proletarian far-right organizations like the National Front: its members held to the notion of white racial superiority, they believed in repatriation and they argued that the mixing of cultures would lead to the degeneration of British culture. Ajeeb argued that they used the rhetoric of 'culture' and 'religion' and 'nationhood' as a fig-leaf; in the end they wished to defend a mythical idea of white culture. Honeyford was associated with the New Right, and what he and people like him wanted, Ajeeb said, was for Asians to behave exactly like the whites. And if they didn't do this, they should leave.

This movement known as the New Right is grouped around the Conservative Philosophy Group and the *Salisbury Review*, the magazine that published Honeyford's article. The group is a loose affiliation of individuals with similar views. A number of them are graduates of Peterhouse, Cambridge. These include John Vincent, Professor of History at Bristol University, who writes a weekly column for the *Sun*; Colin Welch, a columnist for the *Spectator*.

Like a lot of people in Bradford, Ajeeb became agitated on the subject of the New Right and Honeyford's relationship with it. But how important was it? What did the views of a few extremists really matter? So what if they wrote for influential papers? At least they weren't on the street wearing boots. But the ideas expressed by Honeyford had split Bradford apart. These ideas were alive and active in the city, entering into arguments about education, housing, citizenship, health, food and politics. Bradford was a city in which ideas carried knives.

Ray Honeyford went on Bradford's Drummond Middle School as Headmaster in January 1980. The children were aged between nine and thirteen. At the time the school was fifty percent Asian. When he left last spring it was ninety-five percent.

Honeyford is from a working-class background. He failed his exams for grammar school, and from the age of fifteen worked for ten years for a company that makes desiccated coconut. In his late twenties, he attended a two-year teacher-training course at Didsbury College, and later got further degrees from the universities of Lancaster and Manchester. He described himself as a marxist, and was a member of the Labour Party. But all that changed when he began teaching at a mixed-race school. He submitted an unsolicited article to the *Salisbury Review*, and the article, entitled 'Education and Race – An Alternative View', was accepted.

The article is a polemic. It argues that the multi-racial policies endorsed by various members of the teaching establishment are damaging the English way of life, and that proper English people should resist these assaults on the 'British traditions of under-statement, civilized discourse and respect for reason'. It wasn't too surprising that a polemic of this sort written by the headmaster of a school made up almost entirely of Asian children was seen to be controversial.

But the real problem wasn't the polemic but the rhetorical asides and parentheticals. Honeyford mentions the 'hysterical political temperament of the Indian subcontinent', and describes Asians as 'these people' (in an earlier article, they are 'settler children'). A Sikh is 'half-educated and volatile', and black intellectuals are 'aggressive'. Honeyford then goes on to attack Pakistan itself, which in a curious non-sequitur seems to be responsible for British drug problems:

> Pakistan is a country which cannot cope with democracy; under martial law since 1977, it is ruled by a military tyrant who, in the opinion of at least half his countrymen, had his predecessor judicially murdered. A country, moreover, which despite disproportionate western aid because of its important strategic position, remains for most of its people obstinately backward. Corruption at every level combines with unspeak-able treatment not only of criminals, but of those who dare to question Islamic orthodoxy as interpreted by a despot. Even as I write, wounded dissidents are chained to hospital beds awaiting their fate. Pakistan, too, is the heroin capital of the world. (A fact which is now reflected in the drug problems of English cities with Asian populations.)

It is perhaps not unreasonable that some people felt the article was expressing more than merely an alternative view on matters of education.

Honeyford wrote a second piece for the *Salisbury Review*, equally 'tolerant', 'reasonable' and 'civilized', but this one was noticed by someone in Bradford's education department, and then the trouble started – the protests, the boycott, the enormous publicity. A little research revealed that Honeyford's asides were a feature of most of his freelance journalism, his most noteworthy being his reference in the *Times Educational Supplement* to an Asian parent who visited him wanting to talk about his child's education: his accent, it seems, was 'like that of Peter Sellers's Indian doctor on an off day'.

The difficulty about the 'Honeyford Affair' was that it did not involve only Honeyford. His views are related to the much larger issue of what it is to be British, and what Britain should be in the future. And these views are, again, most clearly stated by the New Right, with which Honeyford closely identified himself. 'He is,' Honeyford said of Roger Scruton, the high Tory editor of the *Salisbury Review*, 'the most brilliant man I have ever met.'

It would be easy to exaggerate the influence of the New Right. It would be equally easy to dismiss it. But it is worth bearing in mind that shortly after Honeyford was dismissed, he was invited to 10 Downing Street to help advise Margaret Thatcher on Tory education policy. Thatcher has also attended New Right 'think tanks', organized by the Conservative Philosophy Group. So too have Paul Johnson, Tom Stoppard, Hugh Trevor-Roper and Enoch Powell.

The essential tenet of the New Right is expressed in the editorial of the first issue of the *Salisbury Review*: 'the consciousness of nationhood is the highest form of political consciousness.' For Maurice Cowling, Scruton's tutor at Peterhouse in Cambridge, the consciousness of nationhood requires 'a unity of national sentiment'. Honeyford's less elegant phrase is the 'unity notion of culture'. The real sense underlying these rather abstract phrases is expressed in the view the New Right holds of people who are British but not white: as Ajeeb pointed out, Asians are acceptable as long as they behave like whites; if not, they should leave. This explains why anti-racism and multi-racial policies in education are, for the New Right, so inflammatory: they erode the 'consciousness of nationhood'. For Scruton, anti-racism is virtually treason. In 1985, he wrote that

> Those who are concerned about racism in Britain, that call British society 'racist', have no genuine attachment to British

customs and institutions, or any genuine allegiance to the Crown.

The implications are fascinating to contemplate. John Casey is a Fellow of Caius College, Cambridge, and co-founded the Conservative Philosophy Group with Scruton. Four years ago, in a talk entitled 'One Nation – The Politics of Race', delivered to the same Conservative Philosophy Group attended by the Prime Minister, Casey proposed that the legal status of Britain's black community be altered retroactively, 'so that its members became guest workers . . . who would eventually, over a period of years, return to their countries of origin.' The great majority of people,' Casey added, dissociating himself from the argument, 'are actually or potentially hostile to the multi-racial society which all decent persons are supposed to accept.'

This 'great majority' excludes, I suppose, those who brought over the Afro-Caribbean and Asian workers – encouraged by the British government – to work in the mills, on the railways and in the hospitals. These are the same workers who, along with their children, are now part of the 'immigrant and immigrant-descended population' which, according to Casey, should be repatriated. It is strange how the meaning of the word 'immigrant' has changed. Americans, Australians, Italians, and Irish are not immigrants. It isn't Rupert Murdoch, Clive James or Kiri Te Kanawa who will be on their way: it is black people.

There is a word you hear in Bradford all the time, in pubs, shops, discos, schools and on the streets. The word is 'culture'. It is a word often used by the New Right, who frequently cite T. S. Eliot: that culture is a whole way of life, manifesting itself in the individual, in the group and in the society. It is everything we do and the particular way in which we do it. For Eliot culture 'includes all the characteristic activities of the people: Derby Day, Henley regatta, Cowes, the Twelfth of August, a cup final, the dog races, the pin-table, Wensleydale cheese, boiled cabbage cut into sections, beetroot in vinegar, nineteenth-century gothic churches and the music of Elgar.'

It one were compiling such a list today there would have to be numerous additions to the characteristic activities of the British people. They would include: yoga exercises, going to Indian restaurants, the music of Bob Marley, the novels of Salman Rushdie, Zen Buddhism, the Hare Krishna Temple, as well as the films of Sylvester Stallone, therapy, hamburgers, visits to gay bars, the dole office and the taking of drugs.

Merely by putting these two, rather arbitrary, lists side by side, it is possible to see the kinds of changes that have occurred in Britain since the end of the war. It is the first list, Eliot's list, that represents the New Right's vision of England. And for them unity can only be maintained by opposing those seen to be outside the culture. In an Oxbridge common-room, there is order, tradition, a settled way of doing things. Outside there is chaos: there are the barbarians and philistines.

Among all the talk of unity on the New Right, there is no sense of the vast differences in attitude, life-style and belief, or in class, race and sexual preference, that *already* exist in British society: the differences between those in work and those out of it; between those who have families and those who don't; and, important, between those who live in the North and those in the South. Sometimes, especially in the poor white areas of Bradford where there is so much squalor, poverty and manifest desperation, I could have been in another country. This was not anything like the south of England.

And of course from the New Right's talk of unity, we get no sense of the racism all black people face in Britain: the violence, abuse and discrimination in jobs, housing, policing and political life. In 1985 in Bradford there were 111 recorded incidents of racist attacks on Asians, and in the first three months of 1986 there were seventy-nine.

But how cold they are, these words: 'in the first three months of 1986 there were seventy-nine'. They describe an Asian man being slashed in a pub by a white gang. Or they describe a Friday evening last April when a taxi company known to employ Asian drivers received a 'block booking' for six cabs to collect passengers at the Jack and Jill Nightclub. Mohammed Saeed was the first to arrive. He remembers nothing from then on until he woke seven hours later in the intensive care ward of the hospital. This is because when he arrived, his windscreen and side window were smashed and he drove into a wall. And because he was then dragged from the car, kicked and beaten on the head with iron bars, and left on the pavement unconscious. He was left there because by then the second taxi had arrived, but Mohammed Suleiman, seeing what lay ahead, reversed his car at high speed: but not before the twenty or thirty whites rushing towards him had succeeded in smashing his windows with chair legs and bats. His radio call, warning the other drivers, was received too late by Javed Iqbal. 'I was,' he told the *Guardian* later, 'bedridden for nearly a fortnight and I've still got double vision. I can't go out on my own.'

Wild Women, Wild Men

When I saw them waiting beside their car, I said, 'You must be freezing.' It was cold and foggy, the first night of winter, and the two women had matching short skirts and skimpy tops; their legs were bare.

'We wear what we like,' Zarina said.

Zarina was the elder of the pair, at twenty-four. For her this wasn't a job; it was an uprising, mutiny. She was the one with the talent for anarchy and unpredictability that made their show so wild. Qumar was nineteen and seemed more tired and wary. The work could disgust her. And unlike Zarina she did not enjoy the opportunity for mischief and disruption. Qumar had run away from home – her father was a barrister – and worked as a stripper on the Soho circuit, pretending to be Spanish. Zarina had worked as a kissogram. Neither had made much money until they identified themselves as Pakistani Muslims who stripped and did a lesbian double-act. They'd discovered a talent and an audience for it.

The atmosphere was febrile and overwrought. The two women's behaviour was a cross between a pop star's and a fugitive's; they were excited by the notoriety, the money and the danger of what they did. They'd been written up in the *Sport* and the *News of the World*. They wanted me and others to write about them. But everything could get out of hand. The danger was real. It gave their lives an edge, but of the two of them only Qumar knew they were doomed. They had excluded themselves from their community and been condemned. And they hadn't found a safe place among other men and women. Zarina's temperament wouldn't allow her to accept this, though she appeared to be the more nervous. Qumar just knew it would end badly but didn't know how to stop it, perhaps because Zarina didn't want it to stop. And Qumar was, I think, in love with Zarina.

We arrived – in Ealing. A frantic Asian man had been waiting in the drive of a house for two and a half hours. 'Follow my car,' he said. We did: Zarina started to panic.

'We're driving into Southall!' she said. Southall is the heart of Southern England's Asian community, and the women had more enemies here than anywhere else. The Muslim butchers of Southall had threatened their lives and, according to Zarina, had recently murdered a Muslim prostitute by hacking her up and letting her bleed to death, *halal* style. There could be a butcher concealed in the crowd, Zarina said; and we didn't have any security. It was true: in one car there was the driver and me, and in another there was a female Indian journalist, with two slight Pakistani lads who could have been students.

We came to a row of suburban semi-detached houses with gardens: the street was silent, frozen. If only the neighbours knew. We were greeted by a buoyant middle-aged Muslim man with a round, smiling face. He was clearly anxious but relieved to see us, as he had helped to arrange the evening. It was he, presumably, who had extracted the thirty pounds a head, from which he would pay the girls and take his own cut.

He shook our hands and then, when the front door closed behind us, he snatched at Qumar's arse, pulled her towards him and rubbed his crotch against her. She didn't resist or flinch but she did look away, as if wishing she were somewhere else, as if this wasn't her.

The house was not vulgar, only dingy and virtually bare, with white walls, grimy white plastic armchairs, a brown fraying carpet and a wall-mounted gas fire. The ground floor had been knocked into one long, narrow over-lit room. This unelaborated space was where the women would perform. The upstairs rooms were rented to students.

The men, a third of them Sikh and the rest Muslim, had been waiting for hours and had been drinking. But the atmosphere was benign. No one seemed excited as they stood, many of them in suits and ties, eating chicken curry, black peas and rice from plastic plates. There was none of the aggression of the English lad.

Zarina was the first to dance. Her costume was green and gold, with bells strapped to her ankles; she had placed the big tape-player on the floor beside her. If it weren't for the speed of the music and her jerky, almost inelegant movements, we might have been witnessing a cultural event at the Commonwealth

Institute. But Zarina was tense, haughty, unsmiling. She feared Southall. The men stood inches from her, leaning against the wall. They could touch her when they wanted to. And from the moment she began they reached out to pinch or stroke her. But they didn't know what Zarina might do in return.

At the end of the room stood a fifty-year-old six-foot Sikh, an ecstatic look on his face, swaying to the music, wiggling his hips at Zarina. Zarina, who was tiny but strong and fast, suddenly ran at the Sikh, threateningly, as if she were going to tackle him. She knocked into him, but he didn't fall, and she then appeared to be climbing up him. She wrestled off his tweed jacket and threw it down. He complied. He was enjoying this. He pulled off his shirt and she dropped to her knees, jerking down his trousers and pants. His stomach fell out of his clothes – suddenly, like a suitcase falling off the top of a wardrobe. The tiny button of his penis shrank. Zarina wrapped her legs around his waist and beat her hands on his shoulders. The Sikh danced, and the others clapped and cheered. Then he plucked off his turban and threw it into the air, a balding man with his few strands of hair drawn into a frizzy bun.

Zarina was then grabbed from behind. It was the mild, buoyant man who had greeted us at the door. He pulled his trousers off and stood in his blue and white spotted boxer shorts. He began to gyrate against Zarina.

And then she was gone, slipping away as if greased from the bottom of the scrum, out of the door and upstairs to Qumar. The music ended, and the big Sikh, still naked, was putting his turban back on. Another Sikh looked at him disapprovingly; a younger one laughed. The men fetched more drinks. They were pleased and exhilarated, as if they'd survived a fight. The door-greeter walked around in his shorts and shoes.

After a break, Zarina and Qumar returned for another set, this time in black bra and pants. The music was even faster. I noticed that the door-greeter was in a strange state. He had been relaxed, even a little glazed, but now, as the women danced, he was rigid with excitement, chattering to the man next to him, and then to himself, until finally his words became a kind of chant. 'We are hypocrite Muslims,' he was saying. 'We are hypocrite Muslims,' – again and again, causing the man near him to move away.

Zarina's assault on the Sikh and on some of the other, more reluctant men had broken that line that separated spectator from performer. The men had come to see the women. They hadn't anticipated having their pants pulled around their ankles and their cocks revealed to other men. But it was Zarina's intention to round on the men, not turn them on – to humiliate and frighten them. This was part of the act.

The confirmed spectators were now grouped in the kitchen behind a table: the others joined in on the floor. Qumar and Zarina removed their tops. The young and friendly man who owned the house was sitting next to me, exultant. He thought I was the women's manager and he said in my ear: 'They are fantastic, this is out of this world! I have never seen anything like this before – what a beef! Get me two more girls for Wednesday and four for Saturday.' But things were getting out of hand. The centre of the room was starting to resemble a playground fight, a bundle, a children's party. The landlord, panicking, was attempting to separate the men and the two women. He told me to help.

An older man, another Sikh, the oldest man in the room, had been sitting in an armchair from which he reached out occasionally to nip Zarina's breasts. But now he was on the floor – I don't know how – and Zarina was on his head, Qumar was squatting on his stomach with her hand inside his trousers. It didn't seem like a game any more, and people were arguing. The landlord was saying to me. 'This man, he's a respectable man, he's the richest man, one of the best known in Southall, he's an old man . . .' Zarina and Qumar were stripping him. Other men, having lost their tempers, were attempting to drag the women away.

The old man was helped to his feet. He was breathing heavily, as if about to have a seizure. He was trying to stop himself from crying. His turban had been dislodged and chicken curry and rice had been smeared over him, which he was trying to brush off.

There was still the final part of the show. For this, the men sat cross-legged on the floor to watch the women pretend to have sex with each other. One man got down on his knees as if he were checking his car exhaust-pipe – and peered up Zarina's cunt. Beside me, the landlord was passing comment once more. Our Muslim girls don't usually shave themselves, he said. He disapproved of the neatly trimmed black strip of hair over Zarina's cunt.

The show lasted over two hours. 'It wasn't difficult,' Qumar said. They were exhausted. They would ache and be covered in bruises. They did two shows a week.

Finishing the Job

It was time for an adventure; I'd been stifling indoors for three months, just writing, which can make you forget the world. I'd escape, go to Brighton where our governing party were having their annual conference. I wanted to see their faces. I'd get in amongst them. In four days perhaps a look, a word, anything, might help me steal a clue to what our leaders and their supporters were like. To learn that, I'd have to look them in the eye, smell them, be there. Anyhow, I was sick of seeing history on television. The camera was always aimed at the prepared centre of things: I inclined towards the edges, details, irrelevancies.

Friends said there should be a decompression chamber; the shock of arriving directly amongst them would jar. This seemed good advice. The decompressant would be the south London suburb of Bromley, where I was born and brought up. Bromley (once Macmillan's constituency) was quintessential Thatcherland. Perched between London and Kent it was affluent, white, Jew-free, lower middle-class England. If Margaret Thatcher had supporters this was where they lived and shopped.

Bromley had changed in the ten years since I'd fled to London. It was now a minor business centre: glass blocks, reflecting other glass blocks into oblivion, had been built around the High Street.

Walking past the houses of my childhood I noticed how, in an orgy of alteration they had been 'done up'. One house had a new porch; another double-glazing, 'Georgian' windows or a new door with brass fittings. Kitchens had been extended, lofts converted, walls excised, garages inserted.

This ersatz creativity is truly the English passion. Look into the centre of the suburban soul and you see double-glazing. It was DIY they loved in Thatcherland, not self-improvement or culture or food, but property, bigger and better homes complete with every mod-con – the concrete display of hard-earned cash. Display was the game.

On the day I went back, a Saturday, there were manic

shoppers in Bromley High Street. It was like edging through the centre of a carnival; it was like Christmas with the same desperation, as the shops were raped. But I was struck by something. These frantic crowds on heat for 'nests' of tables, these consumers who camped for two days outside Debenhams before the Christmas sales – they hadn't voted for acid rain; they hadn't voted for the police to punish the miners, or for unemployment, or for the SAS, or for the police to enter the BBC and confiscate programmes; they hadn't voted for the closing down of hospitals. It was simpler than that. Thatcher, rising out of the ashes of the late 1970s unemployment and insecurity had done this for the suburbs: she'd given them money and she'd freed them from the nightmare of a collective life they'd never wanted. She'd freed them for Do It Yourself.

In Brighton, up around the railway station where the Regency façade doesn't extend, there were pubs barely altered since the 1930s. There were Christmas lights around the windows and kids with pink hair, sleeveless leather jackets and grown-out mohicans lying in fat ripped armchairs. In the afternoons the pubs, full of the unemployed, were like leisure centres.

Further down, as I walked towards the front, my first sight was of a police helicopter hovering over the beach, lifting what looked like a tin workman's hut onto the concrete bunker of the conference centre itself. Nearby, an old man with horn-rimmed glasses was holding up a cardboard sign advertising Esperanto. Looking closer at this odd figure I realized he had been my maths teacher in Bromley. He gave me a leaflet which included a number of exercises to translate into Esperanto. ('Use ballpen, write clearly,' it instructed. Translate 'the men sold cakes' and 'the teacher sees a boy' and then 'send this completed sheet with SAE for free correction'.)

There were police every ten yards and everyone staying in a hotel was interviewed by the police. Even the pier was patrolled; speed boats roared through the water; out to sea a Royal Navy minesweeper circled. Obviously the Tories didn't want a bunch of Irishmen blowing them out of their beds again; but there was also a strong element of militaristic exhibitionism in all the security. Nevertheless the pier was flourishing. There were two Victorian-style restaurants with furniture in pastel shades and waitresses in Victorian costume. (As it happens, the pier is owned by the Labour council; the other pier, privately owned, is disintegrating in the sea like a drowning chandelier.)

On Tuesday morning I entered the conference hall. It smelled of woodshaving and paint. The organist was playing 'An English Country Garden'. At the rear of the platform was a light blue wall which resembled an early 1960s BBC test card, consisting of three panels with three eyes in them: the centre eye had embossed on it 'Leading Britain into the 1990s' Squarely in the centre of the other two eyes were video screens on which were projected the speakers' faces and 'visual aids': if there was talk of a butter mountain then we would see a cartoon of a mountain made out of butter. At the end of the platform was a union jack.

The press sat at six long tables below the edge of the platform along which were yards of fresh flowers. The photographers clustered around the journalists, their cameras on adjustable poles, with lenses as long and thick as marrows.

When I looked up I suddenly saw Thatcher in the flesh for the first time. She was ten yards away in a black two-piece with a wide white collar and white earrings. She looked softer than in her photographs. I could see that her throat and neck had gone; below the golden swept back hair and mask of make-up she was loose, baggy and wrinkled.

I had spoken to Neil Kinnock on a few occasions and he said to me once that seeing Thatcher at the opening of parliament last year she'd seemed worn out, withered, a shell. But today neither she nor her government seemed desiccated. Recently I'd been to a party attended by many of the Kinnock camp. They were not happy. It was Kinnock who had not grown in stature with the job; he was too strong to resign, too weak to win, they said; he also knew this. And there was a depressing thing I heard them say again and again about him: he couldn't cope on television. They would be glad when he resigned after losing the next election. So there was no talk of policy now, just of television; and Thatcher appeared odious on television. Later, I spoke to one of Thatcher's speech-writers, who said she was not exhausted in the least. Most leaders, he said, took power when they were old and tired. But Thatcher was only 54 when she took power in 1979.

There were hymns. The journalists, who had already attended three party conferences this year, were like irritable teenagers, and gazed boredly out at the sanitary, dead hall, only half-full. There were few old women in hats; there were many young people – some young men were without ties, in white T-shirts. The Tories were definitely becoming less patrician, more a mass party of the working class. The journalist next to me was reading a paperback which had a blurb saying: 'David Profit is a coke dealer with a dream.' Another young journalist in a smart suit and yellow socks giggled to himself as he scribbled. I went through the conference motions printed in the handbook. Most of them began with: 'This conference congratulates the Chancellor of the Exchequer.' One motion, from Liverpool, stated that 'The BBC does not always give fair and balanced views when reporting on Israel and South African affairs.'

Staring at Thatcher and considering her unexhausted and un-English sense of mission, I began to think of something which couldn't possibly be said of any other successful British politician. It was that in some aspects of herself Thatcher embodied some of Nietzsche's ideas. I mean the scorn for weakness, the basic belief in inequality and the passion for overcoming. Nietzsche, who hated free thinkers, humanitarians and socialism (which he saw as an ill-applied Christian ideal), also dismissed compassion: it sapped vitality and led to feebleness, dependency and decadence. Compassionate ones opposed the natural and impetuous urges of those sovereign ones, those 'supermen' who lived great lives beyond the begging fingers of mediocrities and failures.

So yes, as expected, there was complacency, indifference, triumphalism in the faces I examined as they sang 'King of glory, king of peace, I will love thee'. But they were not a party rotten with the assumptions of power, slow, bored, eager to dispense a little late and guilty generosity. No, because Thatcher is a revolutionary in a democracy; and she is tireless and will not rest until England, Britain even, is made in her image. In that sense she has a totalitarian aspect. I'd often wondered why, after nearly ten years in power, and with negligible opposition and a co-operative media, the Conservatives were still so angry. It was, I could see now, looking at Thatcher, that there was not a scrap of liberalism in her; everything had to be as she wanted it; the job had to be finished.

At last the Mayor of Brighton, Patricia Hawkes, started to speak. There were banalities. Thatcher stared at her, blinking at a tremendous rate, as if Hawkes had started to read from the Kama Sutra. Later I realized Thatcher wasn't listening at all; this was her serious and concentrating look. But Patricia Hawkes, a Labour mayor, had good courage. It was the sentence 'power must bring responsibility and compassion' that first had eyes opening and then widening in the hall of the Worker's Party. Hawkes hit her stride as the audience listened carefully. 'Think not just of those with wealth, but those living in bedsitting squalor, those waiting and hoping for a job, and our pensioners living close to the margin.' Now they knew they'd been slapped in the face, squirted in the eye, in the opening minutes of their rally, their celebration of power. They jeered and brayed, they slow-handclapped and yelled and their anger was genuine. The giggling journalist beside me was ecstatic; he said it would be the only dissent all week, apart from when they'd abuse the Home Secretary, Douglas Hurd. That did indeed seem likely: Hurd's combination of brains, breeding and a refusal to vote for the reintroduction of hanging would not stimulate the dull palate of the Worker's Party.

That evening I went off eagerly to my first fringe meeting, to be addressed by John Biffen. The room, which had a plaque on the wall saying 'Paganini played here, 9 December 1831' was full of men in dark woollen suits. Biffen, a mild-looking man, a doctor perhaps, disappointed the audience with his good sense. People attending the conference craved phrases to applaud or jeer; they wanted a Tom Jones concert, not a reading of 'Dover Beach'. Later in the week I'd come and hear Enoch Powell in this room. Perhaps the temperature would rise then. Perhaps Wolverhampton's clearest thinker would earn a plaque on the wall, too.

Biffen said that Kinnock reminded him of Gaitskell, heaving the Labour Party towards the centre of British politics. The left of the party would soon be irrelevant. The fact that Benn, Livingstone and Heffer opposed Kinnock was good publicity for him, this is how he would prove himself. What a shame, Biffen added, that the press caricatured the Labour party, making it difficult for interested people to see it clear. Biffen then warned the audience: 'We are a party which favours the up and running. But we do not want to be seen as the party which made a country fit for yuppies.' People started to leave. He went on: 'We have to be a thinking party. Where are we weak? The NHS is under-funded.' Finally, after saying the Poll Tax wasn't worth it in terms of social division, he talked of the Soviet Union, saying that in an altered politics of Europe, Russia would cease to be a global power and more of a European one.

Next morning I went back to the conference hall. Outside were a middle-aged couple with a banner saying 'Our children were murdered – bring back capital punishment'. To my pleasure, Cecil Parkinson was speaking. Clearly the Empress of Albion's favourite son, when he performed the audience was enthusiastic, swooning with forgiveness. As Parkinson spoke I parked myself quickly in a spare seat beneath him and started to read, in this choice position, Sara Keays's book concerning their . . . relationship. I almost wrote 'affair'; but it lasted twelve years, as she repeats and repeats. The Empress had wanted to appoint him Foreign Secretary before the story broke; maybe he would become Chancellor even now.

As – above me – Parkinson announced the privatisation of coal, I was reading of how he and his cronies, in the struggle to survive, had publicly smeared Keays. Jeffrey Archer (who once asked a friend of mine if he thought he, Archer, would win the Nobel Prize for Literature), was then Deputy Chairman of the Party. He said of the anguished book, which Keays published herself: 'Not one of the twenty-seven major publishing houses in Britain wanted to touch it.'

In 1983 Tebbit accused Keays of reneging on an undertaking that she wouldn't publicly talk about Parkinson. In 1988 Tebbit and his ghostwriter Michael Trend, busying themselves in the highest form of self-reflection, autobiography, and learning quite quickly, I am sure, that collectively they lacked the essential gift of reflection, repeated this claim (in my uninterfered-with-version), about an undertaking which was never made.

I read of how in 1981 Parkinson failed to tell the police where his car was parked when it was broken into outside his lover's house. He also ensured that Keays, who'd been selected to stand as a candidate in Bermondsey, was stymied by him in her efforts to become an MP. Another time Parkinson rang Keays and accused her of trying to blackmail him into marrying her; he generally abused her. His wife was listening on the other line.

I wondered, as Parkinson pledged his commitment to nuclear energy, if any of this still mattered. Part of the failure of the Labour party is its inability to mislead, to lie, practise treachery and be generally guileful. For a reason I cannot fathom, it appears to believe in honesty and plain speaking, democracy and fairness. But integral to the Tories' vision of Britain, articulated by Peregrine Worsthorne later in this revealing week, was that a future ruling elite would dutifully have to be an example to the lower orders. The price of omnipotence would be purity.

It was becoming apparent that the Conservatives resented what they saw as Labour's exclusive grip on the moral life. It wasn't enough to have seemed to have generated wealth, the Empress wanted to be seen to be good; she wanted to be liked now, loved even. I could see an ethical edifice being constructed, but it would be difficult for the Empress to pull it off: the only thing I never saw beneath the golden hair, as I sat looking at her blinking away hour after hour, was the slightest hint or possibility of that vagrant quality – love.

After Parkinson I left the hall and walked along the front. I would take in something less taxing this lunchtime, something that might turn out to be a little weird. I chose the Union of Muslim Organisations.

In the meeting room, which was virtually empty, I sat next to an Indian who once owned five restaurants in Brighton, though he only had one now. His complaint was that the immigration laws made it impossible for him to get staff. He wouldn't recruit British Asians, they were useless, the hours didn't suit them; grateful, freshly arrived Bangladeshis were just the job. He was very worried for the future of the corner shop, he whispered, as the meeting started.

Douglas Hurd had failed to turn up, but he'd sent two men from the Home Office to represent him. Like many other Tory men they had pink faces, white shirts with pink stripes, and fat bellies. Here amongst mostly Asians, they were on their best behaviour, especially as the Imam of the local mosque, in white cap and beard, started to recite from the Koran. Another Englishman was carrying a piece of quiche on a plate; as the Imam chanted the verses the Englishman stood stock still like a living sculpture in the centre of the room.

Then Dr Pasha, the chairman, told the room that he and other muslims considered themselves proudly British, that this was the noble mother country they looked up to, that being a muslim didn't conflict with being British. He set it up nicely; the men from the Home Office were listening happily. Then he came to the point. As muslims were the second largest religious denomination in Britain the British government could surely give them more recognition. This applied especially to the law of blasphemy which should be invoked on their behalf. He'd written to the Home Secretary – at this Dr Pasha turned forcefully to the two Britishers – insisting that the film *The Blood of Hussein* be banned, and more importantly Salman Rushdie's novel *The Satanic Verses*, which was an attack on Islam, on the prophet himself! Why are those people fomenting hatred against us? cried Dr Pasha, his eyes burning into the pink faces of the men from the Home Office. Surely a religious attack on us is an attack on our beloved Home Secretary himself! Why are they not prosecuted for racism? The men from the Home Office lowered their eyes.

So the conference was warming up, certainly in the conference hall the speeches were emollient and predictable; the uninhibited face of Toryism was presented at the fringe meetings, I'd been told. But it had been restrained there too, so far. Until, after this hors d'oeuvre, I went to see Teresa Gorman speak.

The speakers at this meeting were in a fortunate position. After nine and a half years of Conservative rule there were few genuine enemies in power to rail against. The fortunate ones, those who could speak from experience, were those Conservatives actually in opposition – local politicians in Labour-controlled boroughs. There was, therefore, an excited sense of anticipation in this meeting: we would hear about life in the Red Republics, perhaps a microcosm of life under a Labour government.

It started off mildly enough, with a councillor speaking of

young minds being inundated by left-wing propaganda. Gay
literature was being smuggled into children's homes. There were
gays-only swimming lessons, he said; there were creatures of
indeterminate sex running the town halls. The room grumbled
its disapproval. Not only that, there were illegal encampments of
gypsies all over Haringey who were being given support by
Catholic nuns. As a result, gangs of youths were defecating in
pensioners' living rooms.

This talk of Red Faeces provoked howls and yelps of disgust;
wild clapping followed. A man sitting in front of me in a filthy
suit which appeared to be entirely composed of stains, removed
what seemed to be a snotty gumshield from his mouth and
started to eat his tie. Two delicate Indian women came in and sat
down next to me.

Soon there was talk of 'racist black shits who'd impregnated
hundreds of white women'. Meanwhile garbage was piling up in
the streets.

'No, no, no!' yelled the Worker's Party.

But the room soon hushed for Teresa Gorman. When she
spoke she insisted that cuts in local services which led to garbage
piling up in the streets were not to be worried about: 'We have a
new way of looking at things. Until we get power we must try and
enjoy the awfulness of socialism. We should encourage it!
Wasn't there a Chinese philosopher who said that when being
raped you should lie back and enjoy it?'

The racism of the meeting surprised me. After all, there were
scores of Asian families who shared Conservative values. Surely
the Tories didn't want to alienate blacks and Asians when
potentially they could be a source of support? I'd thought that
the hatred of homosexuals had, in general, supplanted blacks
and Asians in Conservative demonology. Hadn't Nigel Lawson
said that being gay was 'unfortunate'? I would find out. As I sat
through this meeting I noticed that the next day there'd be a
meeting of the Conservative Group for Homosexual Equality.
I'd go to that.

This meeting, which was in a hotel, was hard to find and when
I turned up, the name of the meeting wasn't printed on the
notice board: coyly, there was only the initials CGHE. I went
down some stairs, trudged through several corridors – under the

whole damp hotel it seemed (perhaps this was the Channel Tunnel) – and emerged in a room full of chairs. The one man there, who wore glasses thick as welder's goggles and had a hare-lip, was hunched in a corner and jumped in surprise as I came in. He handed me a newspaper called Open Mind. I wondered if this was perhaps the party's only out gay, which wouldn't have surprised me: Tory MP Geoffrey Dickens wanted to recriminalize sexual relations between adult men; and Rhodes Boyson has remarked that the promotion of positive images of gays could be 'the end of creation'.

In one article in the magazine, by 'Westminster Watcher', the writer commends the party: 'Although some queer-bashing Conservative journalists behaved very badly during the last election, the party at the national level appealed to prejudice with only one poster and a few remarks: at the constituency level the record was worse.' The paper's editorial also refers to this homophobic election poster and remarks wistfully that it was designed by the Jewish brothers Saatchi and Saatchi who should know better than to persecute people. Elsewhere in the paper, the writers urge heterosexuals not to be afraid of the end-of-creationists: 'Homosexuals are as much concerned as heterosexuals with maintaining institutions which contribute to the health and stability of society.'

Eventually a handful of men arrived; but they wouldn't sit down, and waited at the back. It was quiet in the room; no one looked at any one else.

The speaker told us that the Labour party tried to exploit gays, that all local government gay centres and organizations should be privatized and that Section 28 was unlikely to do any damage to sensible activities.

The Worker's Party was hugging its prejudices to itself; through them it defined itself; this was obviously not the time to expect them to relinquish them.

Later that night I was in a restaurant, at a table with various right-wing journalists and an MP. I started to talk to the MP about Enoch Powell, who I'd seen speak earlier in the day. Powell's was the most crowded and exuberant meeting I'd been to in Brighton, and Powell had been introduced, by a one-eyed speaker, as a man proved consistently right, a man who was not only a statesman but a Prophet. The straight-backed Prophet said, in his spine-chilling and monotonous voice, that he had never left the Conservative party, it had left him. And now, he said, to cheers and whistles, it appeared to be approaching him again.

Now, at dinner, the MP told me that the Prophet was his hero. Since the late 1950s the Prophet had supported the free market in all things (except immigration) and had even been denounced by Mosley's Union Movement in 1968 for stealing its ideas. The MP was proud to be a racist. The woman sitting opposite the MP intervened. 'By the way, I'm Jewish,' she said. 'Ah,' he said. 'Well, then, as a Jewess you should acknowledge that there are many races and your race is different to mine. The English are a provincial people uninterested in culture. And you Jews are a metropolitan people obsessed with it.'

Speaking of his admiration for the Prophet, the MP said that Powell was the living originator of Thatcherism, pre-dating Keith Joseph in his ideas and unlike Joseph able to by-pass Parliament and communicate directly with the working class. The Prophet's time had come, but through Thatcher, who was a better politician.

This was interesting because the Prophet had this reconnection in common with another man frequently considered to have slipped beyond the boundaries of sanity: Peregrine Worsthorne, who would be speaking the next evening. However, for the remainder of this evening there would be the *Spectator* party. Perhaps it would be less ideologically taxing; perhaps there would be some ordinary people there.

But I didn't locate them. As soon as I arrived a young Tory, looking like an estate agent, hurried over to me, adrenalin high, and said: 'You don't look like a typical mindless right-wing idiot. What are you doing here?'

'Snooping around.'

'What for?'

I searched for a reply.

'I said: 'I want to know what is going to energize this party. What it is they're going to offer the electorate at the next couple of elections.'

'Oh that's easy. We're going to privatize everything. That's obvious. The Health Service will go eventually. That'll take a long time.'

'What else?'

'There's the environment. But Tories don't really give a shit about that. The important thing is the moral mission. Authority, deference, respect, that's what we want.'

What I saw in his face, and in the faces of his young friends who had also gathered around me to help explain the future, was power, arrogance, supreme confidence. None of them doubted for a moment that their party would win the next election. They could do whatever they wanted, and with the compliant media they now had, nothing could frustrate them. Why should the slightest scepticism, doubt, or lack of nerves affect them? Labour might huff and puff over the intricacies of its defence policy but it was all irrelevant; the left handed Britain over to Thatcher long ago and, that night, it seemed unlikely they would win it back for a long time.

I left the drinks party thinking I'd never see that particular Tory ever again. But the next day, before I was to go and hear Peregrine Worsthorne perform at a fringe meeting and talk about authority, discipline and its relation to the servant problem, I did see the Tory again, much to my surprise.

There was a demonstration across the road from the conference centre, a place now referred to as the Island, or the Island of the Mighty. About a thousand people, most of them young, had gathered; in their tight jeans and knitted sweaters and DMs, most of them, boys and girls alike, with long hair, they chanted and waved a variety of banners for 'Troops Out' and 'Stop Animal Experiments'. In the crowd I noticed an older man with a handpainted sign, carefully done: on it he'd painted two words, one beneath the other: She Lies. As I was looking at the demonstration I glanced across the road and there he was, the Tory with the soul and suit of an estate agent.

He was leaning as far as he could over the crash barrier outside the hall, looking towards the demonstration. And he had extracted his wallet from his inside pocket; he was waving it at the kids, who were virtually his contemporaries, waving and screaming. Around him, other Tories, bored with the conference, too, or emerging from a debate, quickly returned to the hall to collect Union Jacks which, in a mass, they fluttered and poked at the kids.

As the demonstration dispersed, I noticed an old couple with a banner saying 'Justice for Pensioners'. As a group of Tories walked past them, one of the group, no spring chicken himself, chucked a handful of change at the pensioner's feet.

For Worsthorne the hall was full. Tonight it was an upmarket crowd, with Lord Weidenfeld, Paul Johnson and the editor of the *Spectator* in the audience. The tone of the evening was exultance in the fact that Worsthorne, unlike most of the cabinet, had the guts to articulate those things which others would only admit in whispers. Earlier there had been, for example, Lawson's 'I am in favour of wealth being passed from generation to generation,' and Baker's talk of the 'civilizing mission' and 'discipline'. But nothing like this, nothing so plain, so gloriously reactionary.

Worsthorne's argument was that England's egalitarian age had now, thank God, finally passed. The moment of its passing was the crushing of the miners' strike – a historic victory for the Tories. Britain would be, once more, a country in which wealth – property – would be inherited. This passing of new wealth to children would no longer be a privilege entirely of the very rich. Many of those who passed on this wealth would be yuppies; they would be vulgar, which was not surprising in the age of the common man where there were no established criteria for behaviour. In a few generations these people would gain noble values. But with the restoration of strict hierarchy the ruling class would once more exercise a civilizing influence on the lower orders. Others would want to imitate them in manners, speech, education. The freshly re-established and confident ruling class would be the custodians of values and institutions.

The woman in front of me was trembling with excitement at this. 'He's right, he's right!' she repeated. 'Bring back snobbery!'

After he finished his lecture and responded to questions, Worsthorne talked of the importance of the middle class having servants. Not 'helps' which were usually other middle class people – the middle class merely educating each other – but lower-class people who would be cooks, gardeners, butlers, and would find working in great houses a civilizing influence.

That night, as I strolled through Brighton and saw the kids skateboarding in the deserted shopping centre – most of Brighton seemed deserted for the conference, as people had gone away to avoid it – I thought of them polishing pepperpots in the houses of the cabinet, some of whose children were heroin addicts. But I didn't want to think about any of this. Drinking now, I collapsed in one of the older hotels and watched Tories meeting in the bar before they went off to Thatcher's birthday party.

One woman wore a light blue sparkling mohair jumper; a man in evening dress wore trousers far too short and scruffy day shoes; another woman wore a turquoise sequined dress with a great Marks and Spencer overcoat on top. The young people wore cheap clothes and had cheap haircuts; they were brittle and gauche. I could see that for people like Worsthorne a Tory meritocracy wasn't enough. You didn't want the overthrow of egalitarianism, a new economic dynamic, the primacy of the market, the entire Thatcher miracle itself merely giving birth to a reinvigorated ruling class composed of Norman Tebbits, the kind of people who took out their wallets in public and thought Burke was a term of abuse. No; the Tory Party had barely started on its road to re-establishing former inequalities. Money wasn't enough; next would come a confident, rich establishment with power and influence and even better – authority, served by a respectful working class. At least in the hysterical, forced, undiluted atmosphere at the party conference that was the idea.

Tonight how would I celebrate Thatcher's birthday? I hadn't been invited to the ball; I'd go to the Zap Club instead, which promised Frenzee and pure wild Acid House.

I walked past the crowds of police towards the beach. At random, cars were being stopped and searched. Brighton's Zap Club was apparently well known in London. The kids would go to Brighton on the last train and return home early in the morning on the milk train. The club was on the edge of the beach, in two tunnels bored under the road, neither of them much bigger than railway carriages. In the entrance was a small shop selling badges, T-shirts, paper fans. Further in, under fluorescent lighting, the people dancing wore white, some of the men with red scarves over their heads. Other men had long curly hair, which looked permed, and they wore vividly patterned shorts like American tourists. (In fact the whole style originated in Ibiza and other Spanish holiday resorts where you dress lightly and brightly.)

The long passages inside the tunnels were painted like terracotta Egyptian friezes, on the floor were stencilled emblems from the sixties – the word 'love' was prominent.

The dancers were young, around sixteen or seventeen, and not one of them would have seen the Pink Fairies at the Roundhouse in 1968 from where their light-show had been lifted. As I leaned against a wall drinking, it seemed that this was more of a parody of the sixties than a real impulse connected with rebellion. The sixties and its liberations were blown to bits but its fripperies had re-emerged as style, as mere dressing-up. Nonetheless, few of the kids looked as if they'd willingly endure a spell in Peregrine Worsthorne's house listening to him discuss the hideous spectacle of people sprawling on the Northern line with their legs apart.

The next day Thatcher's fans took their seats early for the Empress's big speech. They had their Thatcher mugs, spoons, thimbles, teacosies and photographs in their laps. I'd been in and out of the hall all week but most of the audience had been there all along, listening to speeches for about thirty hours. Now the front bank of seats was occupied ninety minutes before Thatcher was due to start. The blue flags, the Union Jacks were unfurled; some people held up Thatcher/Bush posters. There was jigging and dancing in the aisles. 'Jerusalem' was sung. I must have heard the phrase 'England's green and pleasant land' at least three times a day in the past week.

The cabinet marched on to the platform. Thatcher was introduced. A curtain moved; she and Denis came on; the crystal voice of the Empress began. She recited her speech-writer's jokes without smiling, as if she were reading from the *Critique of Pure Reason*. There was some Dickens, everyone belonged to them now: 'Fog, fog everywhere.' I'd heard that America's finest speechwriter had been flown in to assist. The Empress's speeches were cobbled together like American films, by four or five people. There was much baby-language. 'All elections matter. But some matter more than others.' 'We are all too young to put our feet up.' 'Yes, our children can travel to see the treasures and wonders of the world.'

None of it mattered to the fans. It was the old familiar songs they liked best. They chanted: 'Ten more years.'

On the way out I heard one woman lamenting to another: 'I wish there'd been balloons. Next year they'll have balloons because I'm going to write to them about it. Thousands of balloons, falling all over us.'